Books by Abigail Hilton

<u>The Eve and Malachi Series</u>
Feeding Malachi
Malachi and the Ghost Kitten
Malachi and the Deadly Pool
Malachi and the Secret Menagerie
Malachi and the Twilight Zoo
Malachi and the Dragon

<u>The Prophet of Panamindorah Trilogy</u>
Fauns and Filinians
Wolflings and Wizards
Fire and Flood

<u>Other Books</u>
Hunters Unlucky
Lullaby and Other Stories from Lidian

D1259096

LULLABY

AND OTHER STORIES FROM LIDIAN

a Hunters Universe Collection

ABIGAIL HILTON

Pavonine
Books

Cover Art by Iben Krutt
Map, Logo, and Design by Jeff McDowall
A product of Pavonine Books

For Morgan, who kept asking.

And for William, who sent me maps.

Table of Contents

THE ISLAND OF LIDIAN

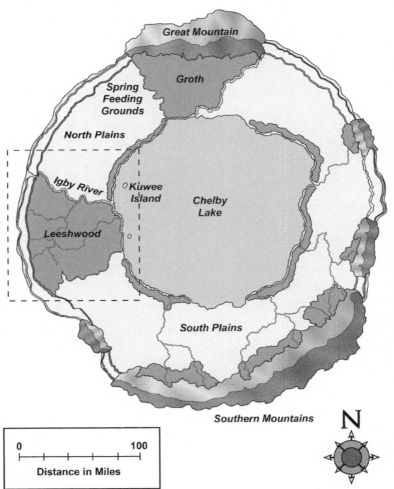

Great Mountain

Groth

Spring
Feeding
Grounds

North Plains

Igby River

Kuwee
Island

Chelby
Lake

Leeshwood

South Plains

Southern Mountains

N

0   100

Distance in Miles

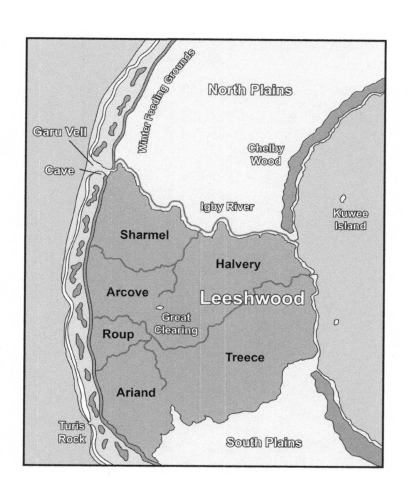

Awake

Keesha woke from a deep dream—deep, deep, among the roots of the mountain, where the earth bled ribbons of fire and the ocean ran through telshee fur like song. She had been young, then, and Kos had swum with her into the channels of night, where everything changed, even their bodies. And yet, they were always themselves.

"Keesha!"

The voice tripped a deep chord in his head—a chord he'd set there himself not so long ago. Keesha opened one eye. The dim world fluttered into focus.

Arcove stood belly-deep in the water of the Dreaming Sea, lit from below by the phosphorescence of acriss. His green eyes caught the green glow, and he bristled everywhere he wasn't wet. He looked like a monster out of fever dreams.

Keesha raised his head and yawned. "Tell me I'm still dreaming and my oldest enemy has not found his way into this most sacred of telshee havens." *And then tell me how desperate you are. I'd like to hear that part.*

Arcove's ears lay flat against his head. He'd been calling to Keesha from a good six paces away. Now he backed up even farther, half-swimming, nearly tripping on coral and the slick rock floor. "I would not be here if it weren't important."

Keesha looked around, blinking. The Dreaming Sea appeared peaceful as always, full of the melodic hum of enormous, ancient telshees, who slept forever in the gently moving water. Cords of light danced on the cave walls, disappearing into the immense height of the ceiling. Stalactites and stalagmites had merged to form columns throughout the cave and fantastic lattices of rocky crystal.

All of this seemed comforting to a telshee, but Keesha was aware that it must seem intimidating to a creasia. His gaze returned to Arcove. "How long have I been asleep?"

He couldn't see any gray around the cat's muzzle, no thinning of the coat, none of the characteristic boniness and muscle loss of age in land animals. *Surely I have not slept for years longer than I intended.* Keesha hoped, but he wasn't certain. Time got away from him these days. *Surely Shaw would not have let me do that.*

Arcove watched the telshee warily. "The last time I saw you was something less than a year ago."

"Ah." Keesha relaxed. He remembered now. He'd chosen to sleep through the winter here, rather than in the traditional deep caves. Other telshees found the Dreaming Sea unsettling, since it implied the final sleep, but Keesha had been coming here for decades. He yawned again. "Is it spring? Summer?"

"No," said Arcove. "It's winter."

Keesha peered at him. "The end of winter?"

"The middle."

Keesha was taken aback. "You came all the way to the Dreaming Sea and woke me up...in the middle of winter?"

Arcove did not quite meet Keesha's eyes. His ears and tail flicked with feline anxiety. He started to say something, but Keesha spoke first. "What's happened to Roup?"

Arcove's anxiety dissolved into suspicion. "What makes you think anything has happened to Roup?"

Keesha's eyes skipped around the cave. "Because otherwise, he'd be with you. How did you get here anyway? I've never taken you to the Dreaming Sea."

"Roup is fine," said Arcove. "He is overseeing the situation in my absence. Sauny and Valla brought me here."

Keesha caught a flash of movement on the ledge at the mouth of the tunnel that opened onto the Dreaming Sea. It was difficult for a land animal to get down without a telshee's help and impossible to get back up. Well, almost impossible. Coden had managed it a few times.

Keesha squinted at Arcove. "You woke me in the middle of winter." He was chagrined to hear an undignified whine in his voice. Before he could think of anything sufficiently threatening to correct it, Arcove spoke again.

"Yes, nobody knew how to find the deep torpor caves or I might have woken Shaw. Something has happened in Leeshwood... in my own den...and I need—" He seemed to be struggling with an unfamiliar string of words.

Keesha decided that he didn't mind being woken after all. "You need what?"

"Your advice," finished Arcove without looking at him.

Keesha arranged his coils more comfortably. "Well, you have my attention. What has happened in the den of Arcove Ela-creasia that he thinks he cannot handle himself?"

"There was an earthquake," said Arcove quickly. "Not a very large one, but a fissure opened in the rock among my hot springs and it…it goes somewhere else."

Now Keesha was wide awake. "Somewhere else?"

"The tunnel winds and we can't see past the first bend, but it smells like a wood in there—a strange wood, not Leeshwood. Sauny said the tunnel goes 'otherwise.' She said that is how you would describe it. She said you would know what to do."

Keesha blinked and settled back in the water. "Such things are rare," he murmured. "Very rare on land. They are more common deep in the sea, at the roots of the mountain."

"That's what Sauny told me you would say. And if that were all, I would not wake you in the middle of winter. I certainly would not have come down to your…Dreaming Sea." Arcove shuddered.

Keesha wondered whether the telshee humming in the cave was causing him discomfort. *It shouldn't.* But he couldn't be certain of the after-effects of his poisoned song. Aloud, he said, "What else? Has anyone gone into the tunnel?"

Arcove looked horrified. "Of course not! Well, not past the first bend."

Keesha snorted. "I'm surprised Sauny hasn't."

"Well, she might have," said Arcove, "but she didn't know about it until something had already come out."

Keesha felt a chill. "Something came out?"

"Yes," said Arcove. "I'm…I'm telling this in the wrong order."

Keesha realized, then, exactly how anxious Arcove was, how much it had cost him to come down here. Keesha lowered his head to rest on his own coil. "Tell me. In order. And you don't have to stand over there. I'm not going to strike at you."

Arcove did not move any closer, but his hackles settled a little. "The earthquake came and, a few days later, a blizzard. A cub stumbled out of the storm into my den, and he was the strangest cub anyone had ever seen—not a creasia, but a cat who will probably be close to creasia size when he's grown. He was striped all over—black and orange. He spoke, but it was nonsense. We thought he must be a mentally deficient outcast, perhaps from Sharmel's clutter. Nadine gave him a little food."

"Ah…" Keesha was fascinated. "And you found the tunnel afterward?"

"A few days after the storm, he led us to it. By then, my mates had realized that the cub wasn't mentally deficient…that there was something stranger going on. After they saw the tunnel, my cats became agitated. The news spread to Roup's clutter. Nadine, Caraca, and most of my mates want to bury the entrance, and I am inclined to agree with them. The tunnel seems dangerous, and they don't want cubs wandering in there. We also wonder what else might come out."

Keesha sighed. "Only creasia would consider filling in an Otherway just because they don't understand it."

Arcove glared at him. "I have not filled it in *yet.*"

"You want my opinion about that?"

"No, I'm not finished. We tried to get the strange cub to go back the way he'd come, but he didn't want to. When some of my cats began filling in the entrance, he became agitated and he... *changed.*"

Keesha cocked his head. "Changed how?"

"He turned into something like a human."

Keesha went completely still. Arcove watched him, waiting. "Well..." said the telshee after a long moment. "That is interesting."

"This happened earlier today," continued Arcove. "He is sitting in the mouth of the cave. No one has dared to go near him. We can't talk to him. He doesn't look dangerous, but who knows what form he might take next? I think he must be like a larval insect, and this may not be his final shape."

Keesha smiled. "A reasonable conclusion, though almost certainly wrong."

"Who knows what else might emerge from the tunnel at his back?" continued Arcove. "So I have come to speak to you. Should we kill him? Should we fill in the tunnel? How dangerous is this Otherway and its creatures?"

Keesha considered. "You were right to come looking for me," he said at last. "Sauny was right to bring you." He stretched, alarming Arcove by raising a coil out of the water behind him. "I think I had better come and have a word with this cub."

Arcove looked confused. "The sounds he makes are not like any language on Lidian."

"Nevertheless," said Keesha coolly.

"Sauny did not think you would actually leave the Dreaming Sea. She thought you would simply advise a course of action."

Keesha rolled his eyes. "Sauny is not a perfect predictor of my behavior. Let's go."

As they neared the ledge that jutted above the water, a familiar red-gold face poked out and grinned at them. "Hello, Keesha! I would have come down, but I wasn't sure I could get back up if you didn't wake. And I wasn't sure I could wake you out of your winter torpor. I thought Arcove could, though…since you spent fifteen years down here thinking about him."

She was correct, but Keesha was not about to admit it. "Do you need help getting up?" he asked Arcove.

"No." Arcove grew still with concentration, measured the distance with his eyes. Then he made a vertical leap to the ledge.

Well, he's certainly not old yet. It was a jump very few other animals could have managed, and even Arcove struggled for a moment on the lip.

Keesha swept him all the way onto the ledge with a coil, ignoring his hiss of protest, and then levered himself out of the water.

Valla was standing behind Sauny, watching the tunnel, probably for lishties. *Smart beta.* "Coden used to come up over the side there," said Keesha, "but I think some of the footholds have eroded."

"Who needs footholds when you can make a vertical jump?" asked Sauny, grinning at Arcove. "I told you he would wake for you."

Arcove was trying to groom his wet fur back into place. "Yes, but you also told me he would go back to sleep afterwards."

Keesha spoke loftily. "A visitor from another world is on our island, and all it has met are creasia. I cannot imagine a more unfortunate diplomatic situation."

Valla turned with a snort. "It's met us."

"Creasia and two ferryshaft looking for trouble," corrected Keesha. "Speaking of ferryshaft looking for trouble, where is Storm?"

"Wintering with our herd on the southern plain," said Valla.

"You left him in charge?" guessed Keesha.

"Well, he can't have *all* the fun," shot Sauny. "You really think that beast is from another world?"

"I'll tell you once I've met it." Keesha thought about waking Shaw. *But she dealt with all kinds of situations while I slept for fifteen years. The least I can do is deal with this on my own and not wake her in the middle of winter.* "Lead the way, o my friends and enemy."

* * * *

It had been a long time since Keesha had left Syriot in winter. The Dreaming Sea remained warm year-round, but as they climbed into higher caves, icicles became visible among the stalactites. When they finally emerged into a snow-dusted tunnel with daylight at the far end, Keesha could see his breath in clouds around his head.

Arcove had had enough of a run through Syriot to dry off and warm up, but Keesha thought it was just as well that Sauny had not jumped down into the Dreaming Sea. She would have gotten much wetter, and this was no weather for a land animal to be wet. Ice was forming on Keesha's fur, but he had a body for diving into the freezing depths, and this was nothing he couldn't handle.

Outside, it was mid-morning. The sky was as blue as a telshee's eyes, and the bright sun dazzled on a white world, bitterly cold. Arcove set off along a trail worn by sheep or deer. Sauny and Valla trotted after him as they wound their way through boulders, along the edge of Leeshwood. Dangerous snow bowls had formed at the bases of huge, ancient trees—areas sheltered by the tree's limbs, now surrounded by drifts so high that a land animal could fall in and become trapped. Even Keesha did not wish to test his skill against such a trap. The forest smelled dark and green and earthy—sharp with evergreen sap. Leeshwood felt as alien to Keesha as the Dreaming Sea must have felt to Arcove.

Keesha spotted the plumes of fog from the hot springs with some relief. Here, at least, was water. "Most of my cats will be asleep now," said Arcove, "but if I know Roup…"

The snow grew shallower, flecked with sheets of ice as they came upon the first of the steaming pools. Arcove skirted it and kept going, around and over boulders and massive tree roots, through winter ferns and mossy rocks, until he arrived at the little river that the creasia called Smokey Branch. Arcove turned and followed it upstream. They hadn't gone far before they reached a deep spring, surrounded by a nearly impenetrable tumble of rock.

"This wasn't as active before the earthquake," said Arcove, raising his voice above the bubble of the water. "The tunnel is around that side."

Keesha squinted. The pool wasn't wide, but curtains of steam made it difficult to see across. The wind shifted, sweeping away the fog and revealing a dark fissure in the jumble of boulders opposite the pool. Something small crouched in the mouth of that fissure, startlingly bright orange against the gray rock.

Closer to them, a golden shape uncurled and stood up. Arcove spoke with a note of displeasure. "Roup, I wish you would not sleep so close to it."

Roup padded towards them around the pool, shaking the condensation from his whiskers. "It's not doing anything. Except feeling cold and hungry, I think. I brought it a fish."

"Of course you did," said Arcove wearily. "Did it eat?"

"Yes…although it seemed to have some trouble." Roup's eyes shifted over the ferryshaft and then up to Keesha. "Syra-lay."

"Roup." Keesha lowered his head to sniff noses with Roup, which was more than he had done with Arcove. *Not that he would have gotten close enough to let me.* "I have come to speak to your visitor."

"I see that." Roup cocked his head. "You really think you can talk to him?"

"I do. He hasn't turned into anything bigger, has he?"

"No. He came as an oddly colored cub, about the right size for a two-year-old creasia. Now…he is slightly larger, but he seems much more helpless."

Keesha considered. *If the visitor hadn't looked like a cat when he arrived—if he hadn't looked like a* cub—*he'd probably be dead. But Arcove has an imperative against killing cubs.* Aloud, he said, "I suspect he is still a kind of cub. I will go and talk to him."

Keesha glided around Roup and approached the animal in the mouth of the fissure. It rose as he drew nearer. The visitor stood on two legs, and it did resemble a human above the waist. However, it had fur on its lower body. Its legs and paws looked feline. Its long, striped tail bristled behind it. Above the waist, the visitor had ocher-colored skin with black stripes like its fur, and the hair on its head was black and red. Unlike a human, its ears were long and tufted with fur. It looked at Keesha with obvious terror, its eyes darting back and forth.

Keesha stopped and began to hum. He chose a melody that telshees sometimes sang together as they were falling asleep—a song of comfort and calm, of safety and peace. The visitor stared at him. After a long beat, he blinked—a slow, sleepy, cat-like blink. Keesha could tell that the song was having the desired effect, so he started harmonizing with himself. The rock bowl of the spring had pleasing acoustics. The music seemed to come from everywhere and nowhere—an ethereal ocean of sound.

The visitor sat down. He was staring at Keesha in glassy-eyed wonder. Keesha came a little nearer. "Now," he said, still humming with one voice. "Tell me your name and how you got here."

* * * *

Sometime later, Keesha turned away from the visitor to discover he had an even larger audience—several more creasia, standing in a knot on the far side of the spring, half-hidden in mist. Arcove and Roup were just behind him, with Sauny and Valla peeking around them, all keenly interested. The time was almost noon, and the sky had become overcast, laden with more snow.

"What does he say?!" exploded Sauny.

Keesha took a deep breath and shifted his coils. He'd grown tense with the concentration required to sing his questions and to follow even half of the visitor's answers. The power of his song had taken something out of him. *I should be in torpor right now, not deep in cat territory, far from the sea in the middle of winter.*

Keesha let a loop of his body slide into the hot spring and felt immediately comforted. He faced the group. "The cub says that his name is Tolomy and he is grateful for the shelter you have given him. He has been running from..." Keesha searched for words, "a great many people, I think, in his own world."

Roup looked confused. "How are you talking to him?"

"I'm singing him questions," said Keesha. "Simple questions— anyone can understand when I sing that way. I can only understand part of his answers. I've visited his world before, but it's been a long time. I think I know where he came from. There's a wood in that world that's thin. A wizard broke it once and it develops holes from time to time."

"What is a wizard?" asked Roup.

In the same instant, Sauny said, "Holes?"

Keesha wrinkled his nose, "A wizard is...something like me. Someone who can sing true songs. By holes, I mean Otherways."

"So," said Arcove, "the cub came through while he was running from something. Is that why he doesn't want to go back?"

Keesha frowned. "That part is more complicated. He killed someone—a dangerous king with many followers. And he is also trying to protect his father and his sister, but I don't understand all of it."

Arcove considered.

You of all people should feel sympathy for a cub who has killed someone much bigger and attracted the ire of his friends, thought Keesha.

"Why did he change shape?" asked Arcove at last.

"He says people with his bloodline can take this two-legged form," said Keesha. "However, no one in his family has done so for generations. He is distressed by his new shape. He can't figure out how to change back. I told him that it is common to change shape when you travel Otherwise."

"It is?" burst out Sauny.

"Yes." Keesha focused on Arcove. "You asked for my advice: I believe this cub will eventually decide to go back to his own world. I told him that he needs to decide soon. Otherways are not stable.

Sometimes, they persist for months or years, but more often, they disappear in a few days. I do not know whether the cub will find his four-legged shape again, but if he wants to return to his own world, he needs to do so quickly.

"He knows that he is poorly equipped to survive here. Human-type creatures require coverings for their bodies. He does not know how to make these coverings, and he has only avoided freezing to death so far because of the hot spring. He'll get sick eventually if he doesn't acquire the proper coverings. I do not think he is actually stupid. I think he will go back."

Arcove looked at the long, narrow fissure in the rock. Even from here, Keesha could feel a faint breeze, carrying alien scents. "So, we don't need to fill it in?"

"No," said Keesha. "I think it will close on its own and soon. But just to make certain that nothing more dangerous comes out of it, I am going to remain here until it does."

Arcove sputtered, "You can't—"

Keesha slid all the way into the spring. It was delightfully warm, faintly mineral. He dipped his whole head for a moment to escape the cold, dry air, then bobbed to the surface again. "Oh, don't be silly. Do you really want Roup sleeping here, trying to watch over it? Tell your cubs I'm in the spring. That should keep them away." *And if something truly dangerous comes walking Otherwise…well, I'm the only one who might be able to do anything about it.*

Arcove regarded him from the bank. Keesha thought he was frowning, but it was hard to be certain in the drifting steam. Finally, Arcove inclined his head. "Very well."

He turned towards the far side of the pool and growled, "What are you all staring at? It's the middle of the day. Go back to sleep!"

* * * *

Keesha drifted from a light doze sometime later to the sound of voices. He raised his head from the shallows of the hot spring and saw that it was full dark—beautiful and clear, with a stiff wind blowing away the steam, and starlight reflecting on the snow. A fawn-brown creasia crouched in front of Tolomy in the mouth of the fissure, talking to him. The creasia's posture did not look threatening, and he'd brought the visitor a small pile of turtle eggs.

Another animal lay a little distance away on the bank—this one night-black. There was something familiar about the shape of his head. *No trouble guessing his father.* They were both adult height, but they hadn't gotten their adult bulk—rangy juveniles, still years away from dens and mates.

Keesha listened to the fawn-colored one trying to talk to Tolomy. The voice sounded soothing. It also sounded familiar. Keesha squinted. *Storm's cub. Teek.*

He'd grown since last they'd met. And now that he recognized Teek, Keesha knew who the black cat must be. *Carmine.* He was one of Arcove's cubs from Nadine's final litter—one who took after his father in temperament if not size. He and Teek had become inseparable within a year of Teek's return to Leeshwood. Everyone said that Carmine would have a clutter one day and Teek would be his beta. They might even share a den. But that wasn't why Keesha had heard rumors about them.

Keesha's eyes scanned the bank. And there, on a crest of stone a little to the left of the fissure, he spied a ferryshaft—earth-brown, barely grown. *So Myla's still in Leeshwood. Interesting.*

"Are you really the telshee king?"

The voice spoke so close to his head that Keesha had to force himself not to flinch. He turned to see a black creasia with golden eyes stretched out beside him on the bank. She was smaller than Teek and Carmine. Keesha guessed a year younger. Her eyes were bright with mischief. "You are making my grandfathers *so* nervous."

Keesha smiled back at her. It was almost impossible not to. "Arcove?"

She rolled onto her back, stretching, completely unafraid. "And Roup."

Black fur. Golden eyes. *Of course.* "I assure you that is not my intent," said Keesha. "It's only an amusing side effect."

The cub giggled.

"What's your name?"

"My friends call me Wist."

"And what do telshee kings call you?"

She looked at him wide-eyed. "I'm about to find out."

Keesha sighed. "What does your mother call you?"

"Wisteria."

"Ah." He was beginning to remember this one, too—a baby cousin to Carmine, often tagging along behind him and Teek and Myla. *She's getting a bit big for a tagalong.* "Telshees don't exactly have kings," said Keesha. "We just have the oldest who wakes. Syralay. That's me." He yawned. "Only I should not be awake right now because it's the middle of winter."

Wisteria did not seem intimidated by his very toothy yawn. She flipped onto her belly again and inched even closer to him. "Do you hibernate in winter?"

"Torpor, yes. It is nearly the same thing." Keesha glanced back towards Teek and Tolomy. The visitor had come forward and was stroking Teek's head with his hand. Myla had jumped down from the rock and looked like she wanted to be friendly as well. Carmine was still sitting to one side, but he wasn't showing any sign of aggression.

"Teek was a cub all alone once," said Wisteria. "He feels sorry for the visitor. And he thinks it's interesting."

Keesha cocked his head. "Don't you?"

"Yes." Wisteria grinned. "But I think you're *more* interesting. How often do we have a telshee king in Smokey Branch?"

Keesha laughed. "You're a brave cub."

"Braver than my grandfathers."

Keesha rested his enormous head beside her. "That might be because I have never tried to kill you." *I have never held you under the water until you stopped breathing. I never made a song that tore your ghost from your body. You might be a little afraid of me...if I'd*

17

done that. Aloud, he said, "I believe I could swallow you without chewing."

"You couldn't," said Wisteria earnestly. "I would be all claws— very sharp and scratchy."

Keesha laughed again. *I like this cub.*

"Is it true that telshee females lead droves?" asked Wisteria.

Keesha considered. "Yes and no. We don't really have males or females. We're all both."

"But you're a boy?"

"Only because I am very old. I used to be both."

Wisteria watched him with shining eyes. "That's so weird."

A creasia rally cry sounded in the night, and Wisteria jumped to her feet. Across the pool, Carmine was standing with his ears pricked. Teek and Myla stepped away from the visitor. "That's Lyndi," whispered Wisteria. "We're in Roup's clutter; we're supposed to come when she calls."

The cry sounded again, and all four of them started running. "Not supposed to be here; gotta go!" called Wisteria over her shoulder.

* * * *

When Keesha opened his eyes again, he was briefly disoriented. He knew where he was, but he'd been sleeping more deeply, and he wasn't sure how much time had passed. It was night. Certainly not the same night. It was snowing. The combination of snow and steam made the darkness almost impenetrable.

Keesha swam around the edge of the spring until he could see that the fissure was still open. *Surely the visitor has left. Left or frozen or crawled into the hot spring.* Keesha wondered whether he should have taken the strange little beast down into Syriot, where the temperatures were mild and he could probably survive the winter unaided. *But he does not belong on Lidian, and he should go back.* As much as he wished the visitor well, Keesha was primarily concerned with what else might emerge from the Otherway.

Keesha couldn't see the visitor at all, and he felt certain that he must have gone home. Then he spotted a confusion of fur deep in the shadows of the fissure. Keesha dragged himself out of the water to have a look. Sauny and Valla. They were sleeping curled together around Tolomy, who looked quite warm after all. The wind from that alien world blew mild and fragrant across their fur.

It's not winter over there. Keesha had not meant to get so close, but now he stood transfixed. The tunnel took a turn and beyond it…faint light. Daylight? How could anyone resist going to look? *I'm not too old for one more adventure.*

"Keesha?" He looked down and saw that Valla had lifted her head. She stared at him for a moment, then down the tunnel. At last, she said softly, "Would you be able to come back?"

"I don't know."

"You'd be leaving everyone behind."

"Is that what you told Sauny?"

Valla looked away. "It would be like dying," she said at last.

"Not exactly," said Keesha. "It *is* like stepping into another life." He paused. "It's easier when you take a friend with you."

"You have more than one friend," said Valla. "You can't take them all. Shaw would miss you so much." She smiled. "And who would Arcove go running to when he finds something he can't manage in his den?"

Keesha laughed, and the spell of the tunnel broke. Sauny and Tolomy shifted in their sleep, and Valla tucked her creamy head back down among their fur and limbs. "Stay with us, Keesha," she murmured. "You have more friends than you think."

* * * *

He drifted in and out of dreams throughout the day that followed. A voice inside him whispered that he should not fall deeply asleep here. He woke again at evening. The snow had stopped and the sky had cleared. The winter wood seemed to glow in the twilight.

Roup was sitting on the bank. Keesha glanced towards the visitor, but Roup said, "I already brought him a fish."

Keesha settled back down. The incident with Valla had left him pensive. Roup didn't seem in a hurry to fill the silence. After a while, Keesha murmured, "This is what he always wanted."

He had not expected Roup to know what he was talking about, but Roup only said, "I know." They looked at each other. "If Coden's two oldest friends can't have a conversation about him, who can?"

Keesha gave a sad chuckle. "I would have gone with him. I'd go now if he were here."

Roup laid his head on his paws. "I used to hope the two of you never found one of these things on land."

"They don't open very often," said Keesha. "This is probably the first one that…that he could have walked through."

"Twenty years too late," whispered Roup.

Keesha had thought he was done mourning Coden, but he felt the grief suddenly like a burning ember in his nose and throat. He tried to swallow it. "We probably wouldn't have come back. But Coden thought nothing could kill him, and I was ready to sleep the final sleep, so…"

"Crazy and suicidal," said Roup with a hint of deadpan humor that Keesha had only recently learned to appreciate.

"Crazy and suicidal," he agreed. *And we'd be walking into that tunnel right now if Arcove hadn't killed him.*

Keesha looked at Roup and tried to rearrange his thinking. *They believe* I *killed Coden when I refused to compromise on Kuwee. Did I?* Keesha couldn't convince himself that the answer was "no." *Stop thinking this way; it solves nothing.*

Roup took a deep breath and shook himself. "Arcove used to have nightmares about you turning up here."

Keesha cocked his head. "Really?" He thought a moment. "Did he have nightmares very often?"

Roup didn't say anything, but Keesha could tell the answer was yes. "That might have been the resonance from the song I was making. Have his nightmares stopped?"

"Sort of."

"How do nightmares 'sort of' stop?"

Roup seemed to be choosing his words carefully. "He used to dream about things that hadn't happened yet."

"My song," said Keesha. "Do you know how difficult it is to make a song like that?"

"Now," continued Roup, "he dreams about things that have already happened. Like you holding him under the water until he passed out." His voice held a hint of acid. "Normal things."

"He didn't pass out," murmured Keesha. "He died."

Roup turned to stare at him.

"I brought him back," said Keesha. He looked at Roup's suddenly closed and unfriendly face and added, "Surely you can see that your friend is at least as much of a monster as I am. No matter how much you love him, surely you can see that."

"Well, this sounds like a conversation about me." They both looked up at the sound of Arcove's rumble. He stalked out of the shadows of the trees. "What have you been telling him, Roup? And why are you bristling all over?"

Roup looked away. Keesha could see that he was still angry. *Loyal to a fault. What did I expect?*

Arcove peered over Keesha's head towards the far side of the pool. "The tunnel is still there, I see, and so is the cub."

"And so am I," said Keesha with a yawn. "I met one of *your* cubs. She was quite charming."

"One of mine?" asked Arcove in confusion.

"Both of yours."

That got Roup's attention. He thought for a moment. "Wisteria."

"Oh…" said Arcove in an ominous tone. "Well, then I suppose you met Carmine and Teek as well."

"And Myla."

Arcove shook his ears. To Roup, he said, "I told you they'd been down here."

Roup sighed. "I will talk with Carmine."

"This time, I will."

"He's in my clutter."

"And I am his father."

"Lyndi may have to discipline him herself."

"And he might challenge her and beat her; ever think of that?"

"I'd like to see him try."

Arcove shook his head. "Have you seen him fight, Roup? You know why they call him Carmine? It's not his *own* blood that got him that name."

"Of course I've seen him fight," said Roup, "and even if I hadn't, I remember you at that age perfectly well."

Keesha listened with his head on one side. At last, he said, "If Carmine is their leader, then perhaps you should speak to him. But it wasn't Carmine who cuddled up to me as though she feared nothing and no one."

Roup quirked a smile.

Arcove growled. "There's another. She is too old to be running around with them."

"Why?" asked Roup. "Someday Carmine and Teek will have a clutter, and Wisteria will be their den mother."

"That is not how these things work, and you know it."

"It's how *that* thing will work."

"In a year or two, some much older male will claim her. And Carmine, for all his skill, will get himself killed."

Keesha thought he understood, then. *Carmine is his favorite. Or at least the one of his cubs for whom he feels the most affinity.*

"Even I wasn't stupid enough to take on a ten or twenty-year-old at that age," continued Arcove. "Not over a female."

"You would have over me," said Roup with a twinkle.

Arcove gave a dismissive chuff, but then he stretched out beside Roup on the bank. "No one was fighting me over you."

"Arcove, Carmine and Teek and Wisteria are *friends*. Not the way you and Nadine are friends. Not the way Caraca and I are friends. They are friends the way *you and I* are friends."

Arcove licked his lips and flicked his tail. His voice came with less certainty this time. "Males and females are not supposed to be friends that way. It leads to...the kind of situation I have just described."

"Well, you started it."

"How do you figure that?"

"They fought your war, Arcove. The females—who'd never fought in a war—fought yours. And they did it because you stopped the males from killing their cubs a generation ago. You taught them to control their own numbers with bitterleaf, so the females aren't pregnant all the time and have more energy to involve themselves in broader politics. Nadine was right. You changed everything."

Arcove sighed. "And now a female cub thinks she can choose her mates. And it will lead to their deaths—probably both of them if I know Teek. He'll never roll over for Carmine's killer."

"And you think Wisteria would *lie down* for that cat?" said Roup. "Arcove, Wisteria spars with Carmine as often as Teek does. You should see them go at it. I doubt very much that she would be a prize for Carmine's killer. I think she would hunt that cat to the ends of the earth."

"So all three of them will die," said Arcove dully.

"I don't think so," said Roup. "Let me deal with them, please; it is my clutter."

"Everyone says it's mine."

"Everyone is wrong."

Keesha listened with interest. He approved of these changes in the creasia social structure. To a telshee, the idea of anyone killing a member of their own species over dominance or mating rights was unimaginably barbaric, to say nothing of a person not being permitted to choose her own mates. He didn't think he would improve matters by expressing his opinion, however. Instead, he said, "Where does Myla fit into all this?"

"Who knows?" said Arcove and looked pointedly at Roup.

Roup flicked his ears. "Well, unless she intends to join a creasia den, I suppose she will choose a herd soon."

"Oh, there's another possibility," said Arcove with a hint of sarcasm. "She might go find a ferryshaft mate and bring him back here."

"I suppose she might. She is quite cozy with Teek and his friends."

"Cozy," muttered Arcove. "I never thought I would see the day when a ferryshaft in my wood could be described as *cozy.*"

Roup smirked. "Cozy." He draped his head across Arcove's shoulders and was silent.

Keesha made himself comfortable in the shallows, stretching out his coils in the deep part of the spring, feeling the tickle of bubbles through his fur. He closed his eyes. "Do you really have nightmares about me holding you under the water?"

No response. Keesha opened one eye a slit and saw that Arcove had gone completely still. "Roup, what *have* you been telling him?"

"Nothing that doesn't concern him."

"I don't see how this qualifies."

"Because," continued Keesha patiently, "I might be able to help."

"How's that?" asked Arcove, infinitely skeptical.

"Let me sing to you."

Arcove grimaced. It was obviously involuntary, and yet his reaction made Keesha feel strangely wounded. "My song would not be unpleasant," he said stiffly.

"No, I'm sure it wouldn't— I'm sure—" Arcove bit back whatever he'd been about to say. Keesha could tell that he was holding himself in place now.

Roup raised his head and started grooming the back of Arcove's neck and shoulders. "Calm—down," he said between licks.

Arcove put his head on his paws and curled up. "Do what you're going to do, Keesha."

Keesha had already started to hum. He let the sound swell until it filled the spring basin like liquid poured into a tide pool. He was singing an old telshee lullaby—a song for peace and comfort, not unlike the one he'd sung to Tolomy when they'd met, only this song was more specifically for sleep. He added a second voice—a drop of color in the clear bowl of sound. And then, because he was showing off a little, he added a third.

Deep oceans, bright with swirling acriss, gardens of coral, brilliantly colored fish, sea fans, anemones, all waving in the current— Keesha saw these things in his mind's eye as he sang. He wasn't sure what the creasia saw as they stared around the spring basin—stared as though the sound had weight and substance, color and light and form. At last, they curled up again and went instantly to sleep.

Keesha rested his head on his coils, still humming. He could sing even in his sleep, though perhaps not with three voices. He had a moment to think, *Perhaps I should not sing this song when I am trying to stay awake in the middle of winter.* Then he slipped away.

* * * *

27

Keesha opened his eyes, but he couldn't focus. *When did the Dreaming Sea become so cold?* His head felt foggy, his thoughts sluggish. *I need to go deeper.*

He was swimming through freezing seas, but he felt so dry. Something was wrong. He had to get deeper into Syriot. Or into the ocean, to the warm, beating heart of the mountain. *Where am I?*

He knew he wasn't thinking clearly. *Need to wake up.* He couldn't.

Someone was shouting at him. *Shaw? Is it spring yet?* Keesha tried to answer, but he couldn't find his voice. He had a mouthful of water. Freezing water. *Why is everything so cold?*

"Keesha! Wake up!"

Keesha's eyes focused. Blinding white everywhere, daylight. Arcove was standing in front of him like a piece of the midnight sky against the dazzling snow.

Snow.

Keesha blinked hard. He still felt confused. Arcove was saying something. He was speaking too fast. Keesha couldn't follow along. His coils seemed to be wrapped around a tree and there were enormous drifts of snow on all sides.

"Torpor," whispered Keesha and his own voice sounded small and plaintive in his ears. "Winter."

Arcove took a cautious step closer to him. "I know," he spoke as though to a cub. "I know you're confused. You're not supposed to be awake right now. Just calm down. Stop thrashing. Can you do that? Can you understand me?"

"I…can…now," managed Keesha. "Where…? How did I?"

"You sang yourself to sleep. Then you wandered off." It was Roup's voice from above. Keesha looked up and saw the paler cat crouching on the edge of a thick crust of snow. Other heads peered in as well—Sauny and Valla and several others. "I'm coming down there," said Roup.

"No!" snapped Arcove. "You won't be able to jump back out. Stay where you are."

I'm in a snow bowl, Keesha realized. The tree was huge and ancient with very smooth bark and no lower branches. Keesha was lying at the bottom of a deep funnel, created by the tree's shelter. He'd obviously been thrashing, trying to swim through the snow, but he'd only succeeded in making the sides of the funnel more unstable.

"Are you sure *you* can jump out?" said Roup to Arcove.

"No, but at least he's not thrashing anymore."

Keesha was beginning to feel acutely embarrassed. "I should not have sung that song."

"Obviously," said Arcove. He was maneuvering around the snow bowl, going partway up the sides until they crumbled, trying to gauge their stability.

Keesha reared to his full height. His head rose easily out of the bowl, although he wasn't sure he could get his entire body out. He saw that Carmine, Teek, Myla, and Wisteria had joined Sauny and Valla. There were a distracting number of other cats present as well—Roup's beta, Lyndi, a couple of females from Arcove's den, several more of Roup's adult subordinates.

Keesha felt a chill that had nothing to do with the temperature of the air. A telshee trapped in a snow bowl in creasia territory, far from the sea in the dead of winter would have been a dead telshee just a few years ago. Even now, the situation seemed precarious. It was one thing to deign to offer help to creasia. It was another thing to be completely at their mercy.

Keesha gave a great surge and flung the first quarter of his body out of the snow bowl, swimming madly. For an instant, he was almost halfway out, almost on top of the thick crust. Then it crumbled beneath him, breaking through to soft powder and he slithered back to the bottom. "Stop that," snarled Arcove. "You're only making it worse." But Keesha ignored him and tried again. Again he failed. His nose leather felt so dry and cold. He was beginning to panic.

"Stop!" Arcove got right in front of him. "Keesha, look at me! Look at me!"

Keesha lowered his gaze. He was panting.

"Do you know where you are?" asked Arcove.

"Yes," snapped Keesha. "I am very aware of where I am."

Arcove searched his face. "Trust me. This is nothing we don't deal with every winter."

"It...it isn't?" Keesha felt stupid. He shook his head as though to clear it. "I'm not...not thinking clearly."

"I know," said Arcove. "You shouldn't be awake right now. You came here because I asked you to. I'm not going to let you die in a snow bowl. Trust me."

Keesha relaxed a little. "What are we waiting for?"

"Branches," said Arcove. "My cats have gone to find some. Just wait. If you keep breaking up the edges of the bowl, it will be harder."

Keesha could hear shouting in the distance, activity overhead. He shut his eyes and hummed a song of self-soothing. At last, a long, sturdy branch shot over the steepest part of the snow bowl. Keesha understood then what Arcove had meant. The places where he'd repeatedly broken through would require a longer branch to help him out. Lyndi's head appeared at the top. "Wait a moment!" she called as Arcove took an experimental step onto the branch. "We've got more coming. I think you'll need them."

Arcove subsided as more branches joined the first, creating a bridge to the top. "Cubs fall into these things every year," he said without looking at Keesha. "If the cubs are big enough, they can sometimes climb the tree and jump out, but enormous trees like this one with slick bark are difficult to climb, especially after an ice storm. If the cubs are lucky and someone finds them, this is how we help them out."

"Well, I am pleased to have been no stupider than the average cub," said Keesha bitterly.

Arcove smiled. "Roup and I slept all night beside the hot spring." He almost said something else and seemed to change his mind.

"It was pleasant?" asked Keesha. He was truly curious. He'd never sung that way to creasia.

Arcove searched for words. "It was like falling into a song. Like sleeping underwater. Song-water."

"No nightmares?"

Arcove snorted.

"They might come back. Or they might not. Let me know."

"We woke at dawn and you had wandered off...trying to swim through the snow. At least you were easy to follow."

Roup's head appeared at the top of the pile of branches, his breath frosty in the air. "Alright, try it now. Arcove, you come first; you're lighter."

"That's something I don't hear often."

"I sincerely hope you will never hear it again."

Arcove tested the steep bridge of branches for a moment, then ran daintily up and flashed over the side. "Your turn," he called over his shoulder.

Keesha took a deep breath and surged up the branches. *I certainly feel as though I've been thrashing through snow all night.* His body ached. For a moment, he thought he would not be able to sort out his lower coils before the bridge gave way, but then the balance of his weight shifted, and he was on top of the crust, careful to distribute himself evenly, and panting in great clouds of steam.

A cheer arose from the rescue party. Keesha saw their tracks everywhere in the snow—cat pawprints mixed with ferryshaft hoof-prints—and the places where they'd dragged branches. "Thank you," he said humbly.

Sauny came forward to lick his muzzle. "I don't know what I would have told Shaw if I'd woken you up and taken you out here to die."

Keesha winced. "I'm sure she would have said that any telshee who leaves Syriot in the middle of winter to deal with land animals is destined to come to a bad end."

"She'd say that about any telshee who deals with land animals at all," said Sauny. "But we both know she's a hypocrite."

Keesha's eyes tracked a flash of orange between the trees. To his astonishment, he saw the cub—the visitor—now on four legs again. He was helping Teek and Carmine drag a branch through the snow. They dropped it when they saw that Arcove and Keesha had escaped from the snow bowl. Wisteria dashed around them, Myla on her heels.

"Look who changed shape again!"

"I see that," said Keesha. The cub certainly didn't look like a creasia—all that orange and white and black fur. The word "tiger" leapt into Keesha's mind—a word from places he'd visited long ago. The cub was about the size that Teek had been when Keesha first met him—much smaller than his new creasia friends, but he was trying to help all the same.

"He followed us when we all went after you," explained Wisteria. "He was shivering in the snow and then…all of a sudden… he changed!"

They started back towards the hot spring. Teek and Myla were playing tag with Tolomy. Wisteria and Carmine kept leaping on each other in mock combat, flipping over in showers of white powder. The adult cats were dispersing, but Arcove and Roup walked with Keesha.

"I forgot to ask how long you can live in freshwater," said Arcove quietly.

"A few months," said Keesha. "It's not good for me, but it shouldn't make me wander away in delirium." He hesitated. "I really should not have sung that song."

When they reached the hot spring, Tolomy surprised Keesha by solemnly laying a turtle egg in front of him. "Thank you," he said in heavily accented creasia. He said a few more words in his own language that Keesha could not follow.

Then he turned and walked back around the pool. On his way, he sniffed noses with Sauny and Valla, Teek and Myla, Carmine and Wisteria. Then he walked into the fissure and disappeared. A moment later, there came a sound like a deep sigh, and the fissure slumped in on itself. A rush of air sent dust and small stones flying. That breath of wind carried none of the enticing odors of that other place, just the ordinary rock of Lidian.

Keesha felt a mixture of relief and sadness. *It's gone. The Otherway that Coden and I might have walked through.* In the same instant, he heard Valla's voice in his head: *"Stay with us, Keesha. You have more friends than you think."* Aloud, he said, "I had wondered if his return might make it close. Sometimes Otherways...wait for their own."

"Well, now the four of you can go back to your territory," said Arcove, his eyes flicking among the youngsters, "which does not include this spring."

"Yes, sir," came the collective murmur.

Keesha was looking at the turtle egg. "I might actually eat that. I feel strangely weak."

Roup gave him an odd look. "You haven't been eating?"

"Of course not. Telshees do not eat in winter."

Roup chuffed. "Because telshees don't usually move in winter! But you've been using a lot of energy. No wonder you feel weak and confused."

Keesha considered this. "Possibly."

"Certainly," said Roup.

"Eat something," said Arcove. "Catch yourself a fish. Or we will. Then we're going to walk you back down to the Dreaming Sea."

"I was roaming Syriot before cats learned to speak," said Keesha. *"You* have been to the Dreaming Sea exactly once. I do not need you to walk me back down there."

"Nevertheless," said Arcove.

"Your great experience did not prevent you from falling into a snow bowl like a yearling cub," added Roup.

Keesha rolled his eyes. "I am awake now."

"For the moment," said Arcove. "Will you come to the spring conference?"

Keesha looked down at him. "I thought you only wanted to see me once a year."

"I have changed my mind." Arcove hesitated. "Storm will be there."

Keesha bent and gave the top of Arcove's head a lick that nearly knocked him over. "I will come to your spring conference whether or not Storm is there." Keesha yawned again. "By that time, I will be truly awake."

Author's Note

"Awake" occurs about two years after the end of the *Hunters Unlucky* novel. Tolomy (the visitor) is a character from *The Prophet of Panamindorah* trilogy. ("Awake" was written as a cross-over story.) Tolomy was in a precarious position at the end of those novels, and this seemed like a good adventure on which to send him.

Water in the Desert

For Amy, who watched this world grow up.

Valla didn't try to talk to Sauny or their two herd-members as they trekked across the arid scrubland. The plains at the foot of the Southern Mountains were some of the driest on Lidian—flat ground of porous sand that could not retain moisture and supported only thorny plants and tough brush. The year's unusually warm spring season was about to give way to an even warmer summer. The bright day shimmered with heat.

Occasionally, Valla turned and looked back just to reassure herself. Behind and to their right, the course of the river was clearly visible even at this distance, marked by tall trees and green foliage— a ribbon of life through this desolate waste. The rest of their herd would be there in the cool shade and sweet grass beside the laughing water—twenty-two animals, including three foals. Three foals where there should have been four.

Ahead of them, the desert stretched to the foot of jagged mesas that began to ascend into the mountains. *Surely we won't get all the way to the mesas before we find his remains,* thought Valla.

Sauny trotted ahead, stopping now and then to make sure of the scent. Her red-gold fur blended perfectly with the desert scrub.

Her movements implied a tightly coiled rage that Valla could well understand. *Why carry off a live foal except to torture him?*

The foal's parents, Haro and Flisty, didn't seem able to summon rage. They were already grieving—hollow with shock, moving on instinct. Towards noon, the four of them stopped in a dry wash—sculpted sand and stone where water sometimes gushed in a torrent before being sucked into the thirsty ground. The sides were just high enough to give a little shade and Sauny stretched out on her belly, tongue lolling. Valla stretched out, too. Her lush coat—so frequently admired by other ferryshaft for its length and silky texture—felt like a curse.

They didn't need a scent trail to see that the creasia had stopped here. The cat's big tracks were all over the wash. Perversely, so were the foal's dainty hoofprints.

Valla tried not to imagine the scene that had likely played out sometime in the pale dawn: the cat dropping the foal, letting him run a little way, catching him again and again, enjoying his screams and struggles. A few tufts of fur lay on the sand, a speck of blood, but nothing substantial. The foal had almost certainly still been alive when the creasia picked him up and continued.

Haro and Flisty lay down and shut their eyes. Valla could only imagine what they were feeling. After a moment, she said to Sauny, "How many do you think there are? Creasia living in the Southern Mountains, I mean?"

Sauny grunted. "Arcove doesn't think it can be more than sixty."

"Why doesn't he get rid of them?"

Sauny flicked her ears. "Because they're not bothering him?"

These creasia were all that remained of Treace's failed rebellion. They'd come across the island one spring when Arcove offered to let Treace start his own Leeshwood. Nearly all the males had returned that fall to rally Treace's old clutter and attempt to depose Arcove. They'd left behind a couple dozen females at the foot of the Southern Mountains, some with cubs. A few males who'd escaped the destruction of Treace's followers had returned. Now, seven years later, a colony of creasia still lived in this part of the island.

Valla didn't think it could be a very hospitable place for them. Water was the main reason. The large deer of Leeshwood could not thrive here. Smaller, tougher animals like peccaries, porcupines, skunks, rodents, and birds did thrive, but they required great effort to catch for relatively little meat. Sheep were abundant in the mountains, but they were jealously guarded by lowland curbs. Indeed, the further the creasia penetrated into the mountains, the more likely they were to come into conflict with curbs, who claimed territories in valleys around water sources.

Even so, why carry off a live foal from a passing ferryshaft herd? That was new behavior from this group.

After a moment's rest, Sauny rose, shook herself, and continued. The creasia was making no effort to hide his trail. *He must think there's no chance of being followed.* The foal, Jet, was less than a season old. He would be an effortless mouthful for an adult creasia to carry. *Or a juvenile creasia.* The scent made Valla think juvenile, and the footprints weren't especially large. *Four or five years old?* Creasia had their adult height by then, but not their adult bulk.

The sun started down the sky, and still the ferryshaft encountered no evidence that the foal was dead. They were approaching the first of the mesas. Sauny stopped abruptly. She cleared her throat against the dry air. "Valla…"

Valla followed her gaze and blinked. There appeared to be a character scratched in the face of the mesa looming ahead of them. It was faint, and Valla could almost convince herself that it was an illusion—like imagining the shapes of animals in the clouds or a face in tree bark. She squinted, looked away, looked back again. The character was still there. "I'll have to tell Ulya."

Valla spent time every year in Syriot, studying telshee script with Ulya. The oldest writing contained mysteries that even the telshees did not understand.

Sauny sat down to study the character. "Who would make something like that? How?"

"Doesn't seem like telshees," agreed Valla. "This is the worst possible environment for them. And besides…" Besides, the character must be many lengths in height and width, carved into a cliff face high in the air. "Someone made it a long time ago," continued Valla, thinking. "Ferryshaft could have done it. Even humans! Everything could have been different back then. There could have been ledges to stand on. Keesha says some of these rocks push further out of the ground over time. The mesa could have been lower back then."

Sauny considered. At last, she said, "I can't read it."

"It's one of the old characters," agreed Valla. "Ulya and I think spoken language changed at some point in the past. We can sound out the old words, but they don't mean anything to us."

Sauny looked at her sidelong. "What do you *think* it means?"

Valla hesitated. "That's a common character. We see it a lot in the old writing. We think it means 'water'."

"Huh." Sauny said no more, but rose and started walking again. The creasia's trail continued towards the mesa. When they reached the foot, Valla was delighted to find a stone basin in the rocks where rainwater collected. Everyone bent gratefully to drink.

"I really will have to tell Ulya about this," said Valla with pleasure. "If that character does mean water, we could use it to decipher other old words. Of course...the basin might just be a coincidence. The character could be a territory marker or any number of other things." Valla checked herself when she realized that her companions were not interested in scholarly speculation.

Sauny sniffed around the edges of the basin where the creasia had stopped to drink. Valla hoped he'd let the foal drink, too. At last, Sauny deliberately left the creasia's trail and started up the mesa. Valla trotted after her. Haro and Flisty followed without a word. It was nearly sunset when they reached the top. And there, off in the distance, they saw him—a creasia gliding through the desert with something leggy cradled in his mouth.

Flisty let out a moan. They were never going to catch up before dark. Sauny gave a frustrated growl.

"It doesn't make sense," muttered Valla.

Sauny shut her eyes and took a deep breath. Valla was certain that she was weighing the relative wisdom of continuing the pursuit against telling Haro and Flisty that they must accept the loss of their foal and return to the herd. They might try to keep following the creasia alone, but Valla doubted it. She suspected that they would accept Sauny's judgment of the situation as herd leader, though it would haunt them for the rest of their lives.

It would haunt Valla, too—that vision of a creasia carrying an almost-certainly still suffering, still terrified foal away into the hills. Valla looked at Sauny. A few years ago, there would have been no uncertainty about her decision. Sauny would never have stopped following that creasia.

Now, though...seven years of leading a herd had taken the edge off Sauny's bravado. Seven years of wandering unfamiliar stretches of Lidian, of negotiating with other herds and other species, of settling disputes among her own followers. Sauny had seen seven winters during which she felt responsible for those who did not survive. She'd witnessed the births of spring foals who felt almost like her own. She'd seen some of those foals die. She'd survived fights, including two serious challenges to her authority. And she'd spent seven years learning to balance individual needs against those of the herd.

Sauny had been a rash juvenile when she stepped into leadership. But that youngster was gone. The adult who had taken her place still had an idealistic streak and a flash of temper. However, she'd learned to throttle her first impulses...and sometimes her second and even her third. Valla had seen Sauny put off decisions for days when she didn't think she was in a fit state of mind to make them. Valla was more proud of her friend than she could express, but she couldn't read her as well as she once had.

The creasia disappeared from view in moments as dusk settled. Still, Sauny did not move. "Why did he walk all day?"

"Excuse me?" said Valla.

"Creasia sleep in the day," said Sauny, almost to herself. "He acts like he doesn't know he's being followed—doesn't try to hide his trail, isn't running… And yet he walked all day with a live foal."

Valla thought for a moment. "If he slept, Jet would escape?"

"He wants the foal alive," agreed Sauny. "He's making a considerable effort to keep him that way." She flopped down on the sparse, wiry grass of the mesa and shut her eyes. "We should go back. This is probably a trap."

Haro flinched, but said nothing. Flisty only bowed her head.

Valla considered. "He takes a live foal, lures a few ferryshaft after him by refusing to kill it, ambushes them, gets a bigger meal for the whole group of creasia?"

Sauny thumped her tail against the ground in disgusted assent.

"We could go back and bring the whole herd," offered Valla. Every adult in Sauny's herd knew how to fight. Unless the creasia of the Southern Mountains had rallied most of their strength for this little "hunting" exercise, Sauny's herd could make them *very* sorry.

"To think I argued in council against sneaking into their dens to kill their cubs," murmured Sauny.

That council meeting, now two years past, had been one of the few ferryshaft councils that Sedaron had attended. He had pushed the idea of a creasia cull in the south, and some of the ferryshaft leaders had agreed, arguing that Treace's cats had no treaty with ferryshaft.

But they also had no quarrel. The leaders who had kidnapped the herd and attempted to give them to lishties were all dead. This group had kept to itself for seven years. *Because they learned their lesson?* wondered Valla. *Or because they were too weak and beaten to try again?*

Valla wondered whether Sedaron's herd had carried through with their cull alone. They did not communicate much with the rest of the herds. *Might this cat's actions be retaliation for something that's being done to these creasia by someone else?* But it still seemed like strange behavior.

"Bringing the whole herd wouldn't save Jet," said Sauny. "By the time we got everyone back here, he would probably be dead and the trail might be cold." She drew a deep breath. "We follow now or never."

Haro's head came up a fraction. His eyes said, *"Please,"* but he didn't make a sound. Flisty didn't even dare to raise her head.

A heartbeat's pause and then Sauny waved her tail, "So we'd better get moving. After a rest and a little more water, of course. We won't save anyone by fainting. I saw some good grass around that basin."

Haro let out a long breath. Flisty came forward and started washing Sauny's face. Sauny backed away with a grimace. "We're probably not going to find him alive. You know that."

"I know he's alive right now," said his mother. "Probably. And I know we're going to keep trying." She looked so fragile.

As Haro and Flisty started down the mesa, Sauny muttered to Valla, "That's what being a parent looks like."

Valla rolled her eyes. This was their ongoing argument lately. It would lie dormant for days, only to resurface again, prodded into life by one or both of them. "You feel as responsible for that foal as though he were yours," she hissed in Sauny's ear. "You don't get to avoid worry and pain just by not having one of your own."

"Do you honestly think we feel the same as they do?" demanded Sauny.

Valla tried to take the edge off her voice. "I don't think *that* is why you don't want a foal." She almost said, *Why you don't want me to have a foal.* But that would have opened the entire argument like a wound.

After they'd all eaten a little and rested, they started off again. The night was clear, the moon full. Valla could not help thinking how convenient these things were...if what you wanted was for a group of ferryshaft to keep following you into the night. Somewhere in the distance, curbs began to yip. The ferryshaft pricked up their ears, but they weren't concerned. Four adults with good fighting skills were more than any curb pack would wish to tackle.

Soon they were going steadily uphill. The terrain grew more broken and rocky. At last, they came over a rise and Valla caught her breath at the view—an impressive ravine stretched before them with glimpses of canyon-country beyond.

Sauny shook her ears. "Well, *that* looks like an ambush around every corner." In the same tone and without raising her voice, she continued, "We're being followed. I'm going to drop off and hide. I want you all to keep walking another hundred paces and then turn and confront whoever it is. They can't be certain of themselves or they would have already attacked."

Valla bobbed her head once. She and Sauny had done this sort of thing so many times, there was nothing novel about it, but Haro and Flisty started to bristle. "Don't do that," murmured Sauny. "Act normal, or they'll think something is wrong. You want your baby back, don't you?"

The creasia they were tracking had followed a worn, switchback path into a winding canyon. Sauny waited until they were on relatively level ground again, then slipped away so quietly that it took Valla a moment to realize she was gone.

Valla started counting. When she reached a hundred paces, she spun and crouched. Haro and Flisty did the same. Nothing stirred in the moonlit night.

Valla waited, hardly breathing. She counted a hundred, two hundred. Then she saw it—a creasia ghosting through the scrub, unhurried, but following their trail exactly. Valla wished she had the eyes of a cat. In the low light, it was difficult to make out details, but she had an impression that this was not the cat they'd watched from the mesa.

Valla stood up, Haro and Flisty behind her. The cat froze ten paces away. After a heartbeat's pause, he said, "Well, aren't you a brave bunch."

Valla said nothing. Haro and Flisty fanned out on either side of her. If they needed to kill this animal, they would have to harry it from several angles at once.

The cat's eyes flicked between them. "Ferryshaft wandering around at night in creasia territory. You're quite the little raiding party."

"We're not raiding," said Valla. "We're here because one of your cats took a foal. He carried it off alive."

The creasia cocked his head. If he wasn't surprised, he gave a creditable imitation. "A foal, you say? When?"

"Early this morning," said Valla. "We've been following him ever since."

The creasia seemed to consider. Then, without warning, he made a feint at Valla, his paw lightning-quick. Valla jumped back. In the same instant, a blur of motion slammed into the creasia from behind and sent him head over heels. Sauny came up on top with a good grip behind the creasia's head. She kicked him hard in the ribs before letting go and darting away.

The creasia lashed wildly with his claws, missing Sauny in his confusion. All four ferryshaft ran around him as he bounced to his feet. Flisty leapt in to snap at a rear paw, making the cat jump and snarl. When he turned to follow Flisty, Valla got a hoof blow to the side of his head that must have left it ringing. Each time he tried to focus on one ferryshaft, another leapt in to attack. Eventually, they would open a serious wound, hamstring him, or land a hoof blow that would leave him dazed and easily killed.

The cat seemed to realize this all at once, because he stopped moving, caught a shaky breath, and said, "This is—not—what I—intended. Can we please… I only wanted to talk."

"You wanted to see whether we could defend ourselves," snapped Sauny. "What do you think?"

To Valla's surprise, the creasia crouched down and tucked his tail. "I apologize. I don't know anything about a foal. I attacked because you are on the edge of our territory, and you seem hostile. But if you let me go, I will take a message to our leader. I think he may be able to resolve this peacefully. He does not want trouble with ferryshaft."

Valla was surprised and impressed. She glanced at Sauny. She could tell her leader was puzzled and suspicious, but at last, she said, "Very well."

The cat got up and quickly put a few paces between himself and the nearest ferryshaft. "I won't be gone long. Wait here." And he vanished into the scrub and rocky slopes.

Valla glanced at Sauny. "Well, that was odd."

Sauny said nothing. Time passed, but the cat did not return. After a while, they all lay down. The moon was dipping towards the horizon. *Not gone long,* thought Valla bitterly. *Is he waiting for us to let down our guard?*

"Sleep," said Sauny. "I'll keep watch."

She woke Valla a little later and Valla took a turn. *We should leave,* she thought. *This feels like a trap.* But the night had almost passed. Dawn was glowing along the horizon. Morning birds were starting to sing.

Valla spotted the group of creasia framed in dawn light as they came over a ridge. There were half a dozen of them. That might have made Valla sound the alarm to run, except that Jet was with them. The foal appeared to be unharmed—a tiny, delicate creature, walking among enormous predators.

"Flisty! Haro! You'll want to see this! Sauny, wake up!"

They all struggled to their feet, bleary-eyed. When Haro and Flisty spotted Jet, they gave whimpers of excitement and relief. It was all Sauny could do to keep them from racing forward. "Those cats could kill him at any moment!" she hissed. "They may want to bargain for something. Do not go running over there! Let me talk to them first."

The foal solved their dilemma by pricking up his ears and barreling forward. "Momma! Daddy!" The creasia made no move to stop him. Sauny gave up trying to keep Haro and Flisty in check. They met their offspring in a tail-wagging, face-washing, bouncing reunion between the two groups of animals.

The lead creasia was not the biggest. He was a sand-colored cat of moderate build, but the way he moved in front, the way the others watched for his cues, the way he met Sauny's eyes directly—these things left no doubt that he was in charge. He shot Haro, Flisty, and Jet an indulgent glance and then ignored them.

"Sauny Ela-ferry."

It was not terribly shocking that he knew Sauny's name. She was one of a dozen ferryshaft leaders on the island these days and vocal in council meetings.

Sauny sat down three paces from him, and Valla flanked her. "You have the advantage of me."

"Thistle," said the cat.

"I've never heard of you," said Sauny.

"We don't get out much." The creasia spoke with the ghost of a smile.

Sauny's mouth twitched. "Why did you take one of my foals, Thistle?"

"I didn't," said Thistle. "The cat who did this will be punished. I ask that you let me deal with him, however. In exchange, I will make a treaty with your herd. Large game are not plentiful in this region, as you know. My cats have hunted ferryshaft before, and they will again. However, your herd is known to us. Let us agree that I will never interfere with you or yours, and in exchange you will never interfere with me or mine. I can promise that my cats will abide by treaties I make." He spoke with a softness that seemed to imply absolute confidence.

Sauny cocked her head. Valla was sure that she found the arrangement attractive. She would be the first leader of any species to have made a treaty with this group of cats. "May I ask why your subordinate took a live foal to begin with?" asked Sauny.

Thistle gave a dismissive wave of his tail. "Young males do foolish things sometimes."

Sauny looked skeptical. "How will you make sure this 'foolish thing' is not repeated?"

"By killing the perpetrator," said Thistle in the same quiet voice. "This is how I deal with those who break faith with me, Sauny."

And there are your claws, thought Valla. *But what exactly do you mean?*

She could tell that Sauny was puzzled, too. There didn't seem to be any downside to a treaty with Thistle and his cats, and yet his words felt like a threat. At last, Sauny said, "You don't bother us, and we won't bother you?"

"Yes."

"I can promise that," said Sauny. She hesitated. "Have ferryshaft been raiding your dens? I spoke against this in council two years ago."

Thistle smiled thinly. "A few tried. I hope they try again. We have plenty of cubs, but, as I said, not enough large game."

Valla's skin prickled. It had less to do with the notion of these cats eating raiding ferryshaft than the way Thistle said, "plenty of cubs."

Sauny didn't seem certain of how to respond. At last, she said, "I am pleased to be on good terms with you, Thistle. Thank you for returning the foal. I wish you and your creasia no ill will."

He inclined his head with a smile. "Likewise." Thistle turned with a flick of his tail, and the half dozen creasia, who'd all watched in perfect silence, followed him back through the scrub and over the cusp of a slope. Sauny and Valla watched them go. Off in the distance, thunder rumbled. However, the sky overhead remained clear. The day was shaping up to be just as sweltering as yesterday.

"That's one cat I'd rather not cross," muttered Valla.

"He seemed reasonable," said Sauny, but she sounded unsatisfied.

Haro and Flisty were still in the midst of reuniting with their foal and were paying minimal attention. As they all started away, Jet piped up, "Momma, where's Ruffle?"

"Who?" asked Flisty.

"My friend," said Jet.

"Is he from another herd?" asked Haro. None of the ferryshaft in their own herd were named Ruffle.

"No," said Jet.

"Is he invisible?" teased Flisty. Jet was one of those foals prone to telling stories about imaginary people.

Jet giggled. "No. He carried me."

Sauny stopped walking. She turned to look at Jet. "Was he one of those creasia we were just talking to?" Jet and been walking with the creasia, not being carried, but Valla supposed one of them might have picked him up earlier. Clearly, they had spent all night getting him back from his abductor.

Jet took a step away from Sauny and dropped his gaze. He was shy, and she was his herd leader.

"Did he carry you away from the herd?" demanded Sauny.

Jet looked at Flisty. "Momma, I want to go home."

"We're going, sweetheart. It's going to be an all-day walk, though. Can you answer Sauny's questions?"

"I don't know," mumbled Jet, his baby lisp growing more pronounced with anxiety.

Sauny looked back into the canyon at the ridge where the creasia had disappeared. *We should leave it alone,* thought Valla. *Whatever's going on here is none of our business.*

Sauny seemed to come to the same conclusion, because she shook herself, and they continued on up the switchbacks leading out of the canyon. They'd almost arrived at the top, when they came around a sheltered place between two boulders and found a creasia curled up on the trail, apparently asleep. Up close, the cat was definitely a juvenile—rangy and angular, thin.

Jet trotted forward with a happy cry. "Ruffle!"

The creasia raised his head. The adults stared back. "Tired from walking all day and all night?" asked Sauny acidly.

Jet bounded around the creasia in the unmistakable bowing posture that said, "Play with me!"

"Sorry, kid," whispered the creasia. "I don't think that's a good idea right now."

"You took our son," hissed Flisty. "Jet, come here."

The foal returned to his parents, glancing between the creasia and the adult ferryshaft in confusion.

"I didn't know how else to get you out here," said the creasia. He crouched with this belly to the ground as the adults approached.

"You might have tried talking to us," said Sauny. "Now, it's too late. I'd kill you myself if I hadn't already agreed to let your leader do it. I recommend you start running."

The creasia didn't move. "Please." His voice was low and desperate. "You know the way to Leeshwood, right? You know cats there. You're...you're friends with Arcove. Right?"

"You want an introduction?" demanded Sauny. "Well, you went about that the wrong way. So unless you want to actually fight with us, *move.*"

The cat got up and took a step back, his tail low, his posture radiating submission. Valla couldn't help feeling sorry for him. He looked so defeated and so painfully young. She guessed he was about four years old—all paws and head, as tall as Thistle's cats, but probably half as heavy, with shoulder blades and hips that were far too prominent under his thin coat. *Creasia at the bottom of the hierarchy here probably starve,* guessed Valla. *Is that why he was hoping to get to Leeshwood?*

At that moment, another cat slithered down the slope to land behind Ruffle. He spun in alarm. "Oh, no. No, no, no, no... They're hunting me. You can't be here. Do they know you're gone?"

"Not yet. Probably not yet." The new creasia was a female no older than Ruffle, though obviously getting a little more food. She had a paler coat and prominent points around her ears and nose. "I told you, I'm all in."

"There's nothing to be in for, except being hunted down and killed."

"Well, then, I guess I'm in for that."

"No!"

Sauny sat down on the trail and let out a heavy sigh. She spoke over the juvenile creasia's argument. "Explain."

The new creasia poked her head around Ruffle. "I'm Kavi. We're running away."

"So I gathered," said Sauny. "Why did this involve stealing a foal?"

"I thought, if you met us," said Ruffle in a small voice, "you might…might help." He licked his lips. "I had to bring you back here. If *she* left, they'd hunt us for sure."

"Because they need all the females," said Valla slowly, "but not all the males." Traditional creasia social structures were highly polygamous. The males at the top of the hierarchy had many mates, while those at the bottom never got to mate at all. At least not with females. The females usually had limited choices. Few males under ten years of age could hold a den. If a young female became attached to a male of her own age…

Valla took another, harder look at Kavi. "She's pregnant." It wasn't obvious—probably only one or two cubs in her first litter. *Creasia give birth later in the spring than ferryshaft.* "Will one of the dominant males kill your cubs?" she guessed.

"As soon as they're born," said Kavi softly. "And if Ruffle tries to interfere, they'll kill him, too."

"They'll kill me anyway," said Ruffle. "Or I'll starve this summer."

Sauny looked profoundly unhappy. "I wish you had spoken to me by the river."

Ruffle gave a bitter, hopeless laugh. "Would you really have come all the way out here to help the outcasts of Arcove's Leeshwood?"

Valla cocked her head. These two had obviously been born in the Southern Mountains. She wondered what they'd been told about Leeshwood, about Arcove, about ferryshaft.

"When I took Jet," said Ruffle, "I thought I could bargain with his life for your cooperation, but..." His eyes fell to the dark foal, looking uncertain beside his mother. "I knew by the time we were halfway back that I couldn't say it and mean it. He was too much like a cub. Like the cubs we thought we could find a place for... somewhere."

Kavi butted her head against his shoulder. "Come on, Ruff. There was never a place for us in Arcove's Leeshwood anyway." Her eyes met his and she licked his nose. "There was never a place for us anywhere. But if we run all day, we might get one night."

To Valla's relief, Sauny spoke again, "Blood and gristle. Just stop for a moment."

The two creasia looked at her dully. "You said you made a treaty with Thistle," said Ruffle. "If you break it, he'll hunt you. Believe me, you don't want that."

"I have faced bigger cats than Thistle," snapped Sauny. She turned to Haro and Flisty, "What do the two of you say? He stole your foal."

A long silence. Haro and Flisty stared at the creasia. "He didn't hurt him," said Flisty at last.

"Just a foolish misunderstanding," muttered Haro.

"You can't—" began Ruffle.

"Shut up," said Sauny. She took a deep breath. "Haro and Flisty, take Jet back the way we came. Run as fast as Jet can manage. You should reach the herd before dusk. Tell Tarsis that I said to give you a little time to rest and then he should take the whole herd to the lake and north towards Leeshwood. I believe Thistle's cats will focus their attention on us, but they might decide to retaliate against the herd later. Make sure the herd is long gone by then and keep an eye out for trouble. We'll meet you at Arcove's den in a few days."

She did not add, "If we meet you at all." She didn't need to. Haro and Flisty came forward to touch noses with Sauny and Valla before starting away. Jet wanted to touch noses with Ruffle. After a moment's hesitation, Flisty let him.

"You're a good cub," said Ruffle automatically and then, "Foal. A good foal." He licked Jet on the top of the head.

Sauny looked at Kavi. "How soon will other creasia be after us?"

Kavi considered. "If no one wakes up and notices I'm gone, this evening. But there's a good chance someone will sound the alarm earlier." She hesitated. "You're right, though; they won't waste energy following ferryshaft in this heat. Not in the middle of the day."

Ruffle gave a snort. "They won't even bother about *me* until evening. They can kill me whenever they get around to it. But her." He dipped his head at Kavi. "They'll come after her sooner."

Kavi's gaze followed Haro, Flisty, and Jet. "You should go with them," she said to Sauny and Valla. "If one of Thistle's cats confronts you, say we asked you for help and you refused. That's...that's what you were supposed to do."

"Well, I'm one of Coden's foals," said Sauny, "sister to Storm Ela-ferry. We don't always do what we're supposed to."

The two creasia looked suitably impressed. "But..." said Ruffle meekly. "If you would give us a recommendation to Arcove...if you think he could let us into his territory...that would be more than we expected. You don't have to stay and run with us."

Sauny looked skeptical. "The two of you don't seem very good at hide and hunt. You're hardly more than cubs yourselves. Come on, we're wasting time." She started back down into the canyon, Valla on her tail.

Sauny wants to lead the hunters away from Haro, Flisty, and Jet, thought Valla. *But we don't know this country at all. The juvenile creasia might be right. We should probably go with the other ferryshaft.* Valla glanced at Sauny sidelong. *You're angry that Thistle trickled you. And this is the kind of challenge you love.*

Sauny's eyes were already brighter. She hated politicking, but now that was over, and all they needed to do was outwit a bunch of creasia in their own territory, while managing a couple of half-grown cubs who'd probably never done this sort of thing in their lives before. *Easy stuff,* thought Valla with sarcasm.

The young creasia padded after them, muttering to each other. At last, Sauny said, "Can we get out of the canyon at the bottom? Double back towards the lake?"

"Yes," said Ruffle, "but we'd have to be careful and stay on high ground. The canyon narrows into a series of slots at the bottom. There's one place to get out near the beginning, but after that, it's nothing but sheer walls for a long way. This is the season for flash-floods. We should stay out of the slots."

As though to emphasize his words, thunder rumbled again in the distance.

Sauny considered. "Thistle and his cats went over the ridge to the east. What's over there?"

"The rest of our territory," said Ruffle. "We use this canyon for water because the curbs don't like it—too many flashfloods. We creasia just come to drink and leave."

"So there's water at the bottom year round?"

"Yes."

"And to the west?"

"Steep ravines and tough going," said Kavi. "No water, except around curb territory, and they dig pit traps."

"Which way would you have fled if you were on your own?" asked Sauny.

Ruffle sighed. "Probably west. There's no cover going towards the lake, and we can't outrun bigger cats. The slot canyons are too dangerous at this time of year. We might be able to lose other crea-sia in the west…if we didn't die of thirst or get killed by curbs. It would take a long time to get out of the mountains, though. Ten days? Twenty? Maybe more."

"Alright," said Sauny, picking up her pace. "Here is what we're going to do: we'll walk in the water for a while, just to make them work. Then we'll leave, heading west. We'll lay several false trails, make it as confusing as possible, and then double back to the stream. We'll follow the water into the slot and get out at the last possible exit point. After that, it'll be a race out of the canyon to the lake. If we lay a clever enough trail, they'll never have time to catch us. Once we reach the lake, we can lose them easily—lots of marshy ground, poor scent tracking, all kinds of little islands."

The two creasia perked up. "But…" said Ruffle, "if they're on the canyon slopes, they'll see us on top of the slots. It's flat rock up there and open for a long ways."

Sauny snorted. "If they don't realize what we've done by then, it'll be too late for them to catch us. Let them look all they want."

Valla smiled. "They can't kill us with their eyes, Ruffle."

Ruffle swallowed. Valla suspected that he'd spent his entire life avoiding the attention of bigger, older creasia. *You must love Kavi a great deal to risk so much.*

After a moment, Valla asked, "How many of the young males survive here?"

Kavi answered. "Less than half. Sometimes the females just kill them when they're born...especially if they seem small or weak. Easier than watching them die later."

Valla grimaced.

"I'm not sure it's any easier being a female," muttered Ruffle.

"We watch the males fight," agreed Kavi, "and hope the kindest one wins. Usually, he doesn't."

Valla remembered her days as a ru and shivered. "Arcove's Leeshwood is different," she said aloud. "It's not perfect. They still fight over mates. But there is more game, and creasia don't usually starve, not even the lowest ranking cats. Arcove sets breeding restrictions, and the females eat bitterleaf to keep from having too many cubs." She almost said, "Cats your age almost never have cubs," but checked herself. "Different clutters have different attitudes towards mating rights. I think you two would fit best in Roup's clutter. It's not very big. He doesn't take many cats, but we'll speak for you."

"Also," put in Sauny, "Arcove will be interested in what you can tell them about the creasia of the Southern Mountains. I believe he would trade quite a bit for that information. You and your cubs can find a place in his wood."

Kavi and Ruffle listened with painful attention. Their expressions of fragile hope were almost more than Valla could bear. *If we can't get them out of here, it's going to be awful.*

They'd reached the stream at the bottom of the canyon—a meager thread of water winding among rocks. Sauny looked at it grimly. *That's not much to hide a scent trail,* thought Valla.

"Let's get busy," said Sauny.

They spent the rest of the morning and early afternoon trying to move as quickly as possible without breaking a leg in the rocky stream, laying complex trails up into the boulders on the western slopes, and moving steadily down the winding canyon. While Ruffle and Kavi had clearly done some sneaking around to be together, they'd never played the role of prey. They did not think like quarry. Sauny and Valla had to correct their technique again and again.

Thunder continued in the distance, and at last, it began to rain—a sprinkling of fat droplets in the still air. This made the creasia anxious, but Sauny only grinned. "All the better to hide our trail. If you want to get out of the canyon sooner, run faster."

As they approached the mouth of the narrowing slot, Sauny made the creasia walk in front. She and Valla came behind, inspecting the trail and making sure the creasia had not accidentally left any evidence that would give them away. The water level had risen, and it churned with a steady tug against Valla's legs as they moved downstream.

They hadn't spoken in quite a while when Sauny said, "Maybe I just don't want to share you. Is that so bad?"

Valla wanted to pretend that she didn't know what Sauny was talking about. But of course she did. *Well, that's probably closer to the truth than you being afraid of loving a foal.*

"Arcove and Roup have cubs." Valla had restrained herself from mentioning this before, but now she was tired and hungry. She said the first thing that came to mind. "He and Roup have each other, and they have cubs, and so can we."

"Arcove and Roup are creasia," said Sauny, an edge of frustration in her voice. "Their species has a tradition of this sort of thing. Besides, Arcove is an enormous predator!"

An enormous predator whom you admire tremendously.

Sauny continued with a toss of her head. "He tells everyone how it's going to be, and they just get in line!"

Valla rolled her eyes. "What are you afraid of? That some male will steal me? That's ridiculous, Sauny. I am not helpless."

"No," snapped Sauny, "I'm afraid he'll steal my herd."

And there it was—the ugliest side of this argument. Female leaders were rare among ferryshaft. Sauny's relationship with Valla enhanced her position. Valla was an attractive mate. Male ferryshaft admired Sauny's hold on her and treated Sauny like another male because of it. *If I take another mate, that makes you look weak. And you value the power and authority you've built. You value your authority more than...*

"Valla, don't," said Sauny in a voice so low Valla could barely hear her.

"Don't what?" asked Valla coldly.

"Don't take that in the worst possible way. I have a lot on my mind at the moment."

"You always do."

It was just past noon. Valla wondered whether the creasia were having difficulty staying awake. Around them, the slot had nar-

65

rowed until it was only a few lengths across. The high walls had been sculpted into fantastic shapes by water. Even in her distracted state, Valla could not help admiring their deadly beauty.

Those curves were shaped by flashfloods. The top of the slot rose as high above their heads as a forest tree. Looking up, Valla was startled to see a log wedged more than halfway to the top. No trees of that size grew anywhere near here. A flashflood had brought that log down out of the mountains and rammed it into the slot far above their heads. Valla could not imagine the violence of water that could do such a thing.

Sauny stopped in a narrow grotto and turned in a slow circle. The walls rose in elegant curves, sunlight falling in shafts from above onto the sheet of fast-moving water at their feet. The creasia were splashing somewhere ahead, out of sight around a bend. For the moment, Sauny and Valla were alone.

Sauny spoke without taking her eyes off the walls. "What we have is so unusual. I'm afraid that if we make it look like something more common, it will break." She sounded less certain now and Valla couldn't stay angry.

"It won't."

"You don't know that."

What they had *was* unusual, but only from a certain angle. Male ferryshaft sometimes took several female mates. During the breeding season, the entire group sometimes interacted. Occasionally, the females grew just as close to each other as to their male mate. Sometimes, if the male died, they even stayed together. The only truly unusual thing about Sauny and Valla's relationship was the fact that they had never had a male partner.

"You won't choose a low-ranking father for your foal," said Sauny with a kind of sweet frustration. "You like alphas."

That made Valla laugh. "Obviously."

Then Sauny was laughing with her.

"But I wouldn't choose someone who would try to take your herd from you!"

"You don't know that." Sauny started walking again, trotting to catch up to Ruffle and Kavi. Valla noticed, as they came out into a wider spot, that the rain had gotten heavier. The water churning around her legs was deeper and muddier.

"How far until we get out?" she asked Ruffle as they caught up.

"Not far." Ruffle was panting. Valla thought it had more to do with stress than fatigue. "The rain is a bad sign; we need to hurry."

They were all running now. It was exhausting in the muddy water, but if they stood still for even a moment, their feet sank in the thickening sludge. Sauny nudged Valla's shoulder abruptly. "Look!"

Valla turned. High on the canyon wall, she made out the same character they'd seen on the mesa. It was not as large, but still impressive. Just beneath the character ran an unnaturally straight line.

"What do you think it means?" Sauny spoke in Valla's ear over the rushing water.

"I think it means, 'This is how high the water comes.'" *And we really don't want to be in the slot when that happens.*

To Valla's relief, the creasia were struggling out of the slot ahead of them, up a steep trail onto the flat, stony ground on top. When they all stood dripping and breathless on the edge of the slot, Sauny turned and looked back over the canyon. Valla followed her gaze. Ruffle had been right. The flat rock gave a good view of the upper canyon. Through the haze of rain, a half dozen creasia were visible combing the western slopes.

"Ha!" Sauny waved her tail in satisfaction.

Even Kavi and Ruffle were cautiously pleased. "They won't follow us into the slots with this rain," said Ruffle. "They won't even like to stay near the stream with the weather like this."

"If the lower canyon curves the way I think it does, we'll make the lake by dark," said Sauny.

The rain was coming down in sheets now, and it gushed over the edges of the slot. At the bottom, the stream had become a river. From the safety of the top, Valla was interested in watching the flashflood. *Will there be logs, I wonder?*

Sauny made her way briskly along the edge with the others just behind. The rain was so thick that she almost ran into Thistle as he rose from a dip in the rocks.

Valla had a sick moment of vertigo as her mind's eye flashed an image of a smaller Sauny and a bigger creasia—Arcove lashing out with his claws, flipping her through the air amid a spray of blood.

But that was a different Sauny, a different cat. *This* Sauny jumped straight in the air as the creasia flew at her and kicked him in the head as she came down.

Everything happened at once as Valla raced in to distract Thistle, Sauny hit the ground and skittered sideways, and four more cats leapt up from their hiding places. Valla felt the sting of claws across her chest, no doubt meant for her throat and face, but missing as she reared. Her lashing hoof caught Thistle in the nose. Then she was backing away, Sauny beside her. Valla spared a glance over her shoulder and saw Ruffle and Kavi being herded against them by the circling cats. There was nothing to do but put their backs to the edge of the slot.

"I told you," grated Thistle, his nose streaming blood in the rain. "I told you what I do to those who break faith with me."

Half under her breath, Sauny murmured, "I need you all to trust me. We're going into the slot on my count. It's a long fall, but we can make it. One."

Ruffle's head jerked around towards Sauny, his eyes huge and wild.

"Shhh," whispered Sauny without looking at him. "We're running back the way we came. Trust me." Then she raised her voice and called to Thistle over the rain. "I have not broken faith with you, cat. Unless you keep your followers captive. Is that the case? You should have said." Softly she said, "Two."

"You are taking those two spies to report to Arcove in Leeshwood," spat Thistle. "The female is ours, and the male does not have permission to leave. You violated our treaty, Sauny Ela-ferry, and I will have your life for it." His lips curled and his eyes settled on

Valla. "But first, your friend. Nothing tastes better than big game, eaten live."

"Three," said Sauny.

They turned together and jumped. Valla felt proud of Ruffle and Kavi. They must have been terrified. They weren't used to fights or chases, and they were hardly more than cubs, but they did not hesitate. When they hit the water—belly-deep now and ice cold— they struck out after Sauny with all their strength. So did Valla, although she felt like panicking.

Valla supposed that Sauny must think they had a better chance in the water than fighting Thistle's cats. Valla had to admit that the fight was poor odds, but the water seemed even poorer. Cataracts were shooting down into the slot on all sides. The current churned powerfully around their legs, but the water in the slot now was nothing compared to what was surely coming.

And we are running to meet it, thought Valla. Sauny moved upstream in great bounds, careless of her footing, throwing caution to the wind in a desperate bid to beat the flood to...what?

Valla glanced again at the young creasia. Their eyes were wild, but they were focused completely on Sauny. *They think we know what we're doing.*

On they raced, through waterfalls shooting over the sides of the slot and, finally into the dark throat of the narrowest section. Valla could hardly see with the torturous walls blocking the sky and no sunlight to pierce the gloom. She forced herself not to think about being battered to pieces against those twisting walls.

At last, Sauny stopped, panting, in the grotto where they'd spoken earlier. The two creasia stood trembling and dripping beside them. Valla could hear something in the distance—a rumble above the rain. "Sauny…" She hadn't meant for her voice to break.

Sauny was scanning the walls, squinting fiercely. "Valla, help me find it. I saw it earlier while we were talking."

Valla looked up—up, up around the sensuous curves of the slot. And she saw… "A character?"

"Yes!" Sauny caught sight of it in the same moment. "Yes, and right above it a ledge. You see? We can get up there. We'll have to jump between the walls. I see three good jump points. I'll go first. You all copy me. Ready?"

Valla wanted to ask so many questions. The ledge Sauny referred to was beneath an overhang. The character was just below it. Finding anywhere to get out of the water in the slot was unexpected, but… *If the flood rises above that ledge, we'll be swept away. We can't even try to jump to the top of the slot because of the overhang.*

But there was no time to argue. Sauny demonstrated three perfectly executed ricochet jumps between the walls of the slot to the ledge. Valla shook her head. *You're certainly your brother's sister.* It was the sort of thing Storm would do, and most other ferryshaft wouldn't even consider.

Valla made the creasia go next. Being cats, they managed the maneuver pretty well. Valla, being more of a ferryshaft in this regard, tried once and failed. The water in the grotto was almost too deep for jumping. She slipped when she landed and went down painfully against the rock. Sauny leaned forward on the ledge. Valla grimaced up at her. *Don't come back down here, idiot.*

Valla tried again. She managed to get her front feet onto the ledge. Sauny caught a mouthful of the fur behind her head and hauled her the rest of the way. The ledge was barely long enough for the four of them. The two creasia were huddled against each other. Valla pressed herself against Sauny, pushing them as tightly to the wall as possible, her head over Sauny's hips.

And the flood came.

It crashed through the narrow slot, pounding against the walls, making the ground vibrate. Something collided with the rock below their ledge—a log, a boulder? The flood brought its own wind—cold, the way Valla imagined a ghost must feel.

The water rose and kept rising. "Don't worry!" Sauny shouted over the flood. "The water character was below the ledge!"

Valla gave a hysterical laugh. *"That's* why you brought us here?! Sauny, it might not mean what I think it means! I might be completely wrong!"

"I trust you," said Sauny.

I *don't trust me this much!* "Sauny, everything could have changed since that character was written!"

"Then it would have eroded!"

You don't know that! Valla almost shouted Sauny's words back at her, but bit them down.

The water rose with horrible speed. It gleamed barely a length beneath them, deadly whitewater, splashing up onto their ledge.

"Who do you want for the father?" asked Sauny.

"What?!"

Sauny inched back a little so that their heads were closer together. "Who?"

"I—" Valla could see in Sauny's eyes that she was not as confident as her voice implied. Valla could feel her trembling. She took a deep breath. *Plan the future as though we have one.*

"Kelsy."

Sauny gave a jittery laugh. "You would name the most charismatic herd leader on the island. Do you really like him that much?"

"I think he's good b-breeding material." Valla's teeth were chattering, both with fear and cold. The water was less than a length below them now, splashing over the ledge, soaking them. "And I do like him. You like him, too; he taught us to fight."

"I suppose I should just be glad you didn't say 'Storm,'" said Sauny.

Valla giggled in spite of herself. "That would be strange."

"It would make the foal my blood kin."

"I don't think Tollee would like it."

"I think you're right."

"And besides, I...I hoped..." Valla could see the churning water reflected in Sauny's eyes. *We don't have a future. No, no, don't think that.* "I know you don't want to carry a foal," she babbled, "but I hoped you'd still be...part of it. Of everything. So, no, not your brother."

Sauny thought about that. Valla supposed they might die while she was thinking. The water rose to a tail's length beneath the ledge.

And stayed.

Valla didn't dare believe it at first. She stared into the whirling blackness until her eyes burned. She compared the water level to other rock formations in the slot. She knew she wasn't imagining things, though, when Kavi looked over her shoulder and said with awe and glee, "Thistle will never believe we survived. We can walk away! And he'll never know!"

Ruffle started laughing. He tucked his head against Kavi's side and shook with relief.

Sauny started grooming Valla's throat and chest where Thistle's claws had caught her. "So the two of us…and Kelsy," she said between licks.

Valla swallowed. "It could be fun…if you'd let it."

"I wonder if he will say yes." Sauny spoke with a hint of humor in her sarcasm.

Valla choked on a giggle. She was still trembling from cold and the fear of their narrow escape.

Sauny stopped grooming abruptly and thumped the stone with her tail. "Storm will love this story! I cannot wait to tell him! I wonder if he's in Leeshwood right now." She sounded happy—not resentful or bitter and brooding. Once Sauny had made up her mind about something, she let it go.

I will have a foal! thought Valla in wonder. *Of my very own. We* will *have a foal!*

The water level had already started to sink. The rain had stopped, and the capricious sun pierced the grotto, spreading warmth and light. It dazzled on the churning flood, and Valla no longer thought of death. She looked at the water and thought of ribbons of green through barren places, of new beginnings, of growing things, of life.

Lullaby

For Hank (Hankus, Hankus-pankus the Buddha-pest), best
of cats. And for Galaxy – may she play among the stars.

Part I

Charder Ela-ferry lay dying on a beautiful day in summer. The
illness had come on suddenly. He'd been teaching his grandfoals to stalk sheep early in the season, when he'd first noticed the
odd breathlessness. He hadn't mentioned it to anyone, but he'd
stopped chasing big game. Instead, he'd spent days in the Ferryshaft
Caves of History, improving the reading skills of the youngsters
who traveled there from herds all over the island. He'd watched his
grandfoals trace the characters that told the stories of their people,
wearing the words just a little bit deeper with each repetition. He
watched them practice their own writing in smooth beach sand.

Charder made the trek to Chelby Lake that summer—harder
than it should have been—with his daughter, because she'd always
loved that place. He fished with her in the shallows, as he had the
first summer of her life. He told So-fet, for the hundredth time, that
it would be quite reasonable for her to find a new mate this fall. "I
chose you nine years ago," she said cheerfully. "I choose you still."

When he lost his appetite at the height of the season's bounty, Charder knew it was time to tell her. She didn't believe him at first. No one did. So-fet brought him all his favorite foods and the wisest of his old herd-members brought him medicinal greens and berries, carefully selected. Nothing helped. There was little pain, except when Charder tried to eat, so he didn't.

Storm walked him down to Syriot, where Shaw took one sniff and said, "No healing pool can cure this, Storm."

"I am content," Charder kept telling them. "I am fifty-three years old. I never expected to live so long." *I never expected to have such a wonderful final decade.*

"I could sing to make you comfortable," offered Shaw.

"I am comfortable," said Charder. "Or I was. Back in the daylight."

"Can we ask Keesha?" persisted Storm.

"He has gone wandering," said Shaw. "I will tell him when next we meet." She hesitated. "I know what he will say, though. He will say that the only cure for old age is to walk otherwise."

Charder shivered. "I am a ferryshaft of Lidian. I will die as such."

So they'd allowed Charder to return to the pleasant little grotto beside the hot spring where he and So-fet had wintered most years since they'd been together. It was on the Southern Plains just a little south of Leeshwood, not far from the Ferryshaft Caves of History.

Charder finally permitted his family to fuss over him a bit. His daughter and her mate brought his grandfoals nearly every day.

So-fet kept tempting him with soft turtle eggs and perfect little fish. He did try to eat sometimes, and occasionally succeeded. But he was losing weight with alarming speed. *I will not make the fall conference,* he thought wistfully. And that was when he said, "Storm, would you tell Arcove I'd like to see him?"

Storm had promised he would, but days passed, and Arcove did not appear. Everyone else did. Most of Charder's old herd-members, Sauny and Valla and their two-year-old foal, who'd been fathered by Kelsy.

Kelsy himself sent his respects, though he could not leave his herd on the far side of the island. Ferryshaft whom Charder hadn't spoken with in years came from herds far and near to say goodbye. Occasionally, they came to apologize for slights committed against him long ago, or for causing mischief in various aspects of herd politics. Charder assured them that he held no resentment. "I don't even remember," he said to most of them. "Be at peace."

He was shocked one evening when Teek glided out of the boulders. He was a handsome, fawn-colored animal in his prime, sleek and glossy. A black cat padded behind him, and Charder thought for a moment it was Arcove. But, no. This was one of his grown cubs, Carmine—part of Nadine's final litter. They'd brought their mate, Wisteria, and a pair of three-year-old cubs.

Charder had met this group several times when he was in Leeshwood. There had been rumors for years about Carmine, his similarities to his father, and his possible future. Young creasia did not usually seek Charder out for conversation, however, and he was surprised they'd made this journey. "We wanted to pay our respects," said Teek, "and to teach our cubs some history."

"We're going to the writing caves tomorrow," said Wisteria, "but you're even better. You lived it!"

Charder smiled. *I am living history.*

The cubs did most of the talking at the beginning, asking questions about the war, about battles, particularly about the fight with Treace's cats on Kuwee Island. So-fet came into the cave at sunset and lay down beside Charder. She listened for a while, and finally fell asleep.

The night was clear and beautiful. Frogs sang in the stream. At last, the cubs wandered off to play and hunt, but the adults kept talking. Teek wanted to know how Charder perceived the herd Storm had grown up in. Wisteria asked questions about telshees and ferryshaft before the war.

Carmine was the quietest. Charder couldn't tell what he thought of this outing. At last, he raised his head with a challenge in his green eyes and said, "What was it like to watch my father fight Coden on Turis Rock?"

Teek gave Carmine a *look,* but Charder answered mildly, "It was hard, because I wanted to interfere and I couldn't without risking the herd. It was hard to watch my friend die."

The cats went very still. Teek was glaring at Carmine.

"But Arcove offered to finish it painlessly," said Charder very softly. "I'm not sure any of the creasia at the foot of the rock heard that part. I was underneath the overhang, so I couldn't see everything at the end, but I heard them talking…right before Coden jumped."

Carmine's face had lost its antagonism. *I've gotten so much better at reading creasia faces.* Charder turned his focus inward. The memory of that evening had been seared into his brain for years, returning vividly in nightmares. But he hadn't thought about it lately. Not for a long time. *Arcove said, "I don't want this." He said, "It doesn't have to end this way."*

"Arcove would have negotiated," said Charder aloud, "if Coden had been willing to do what I did." After a moment, he added, "And Coden would have been better at it than I was."

"No!" said Wisteria fiercely, as though she'd been holding something in. "I have heard you in council, Charder Ela-ferry. No one is more forthright with dear old Papa Arcy than you are. No one dares. Well, except Roup, but he doesn't count. And Keesha. When he shows up."

Charder burst out laughing. "Please tell me you call him that to his face."

Wisteria kept a deadpan expression while her mates snickered into their paws. "I do not. I value all my limbs."

"It took me twenty years to learn how to be forthright with him!" objected Charder. "And he's nowhere near as stubborn as he used to be." He looked hard at Carmine. "You're not going to challenge him, are you?"

Carmine's teeth flashed in a bitter smile. "There wouldn't be any point. Supposedly the council is going to vote on our next king. If my father dropped dead tomorrow, they'd choose Roup."

"As they should," said Teek pointedly. "He's got decades of experience."

"It wouldn't make Roup happy," observed Wisteria. "Being king, I mean."

"It didn't make *Arcove* happy," said Teek, responding to Wisteria, but looking at Carmine.

Carmine rolled his eyes. "I'm not going to challenge my father, because I *like* the old tyrant. I just wish I knew whether I could beat him, is all." Half under his breath, he muttered, "How do you follow a legend like that?"

"With a completely different story," said Wisteria. She turned back to Charder, "Sir, you look tired. You're a day animal, and we've kept you awake half the night."

Charder was, indeed, having trouble keeping his eyes open, in spite of the interesting conversation. "I'm a dying animal, and I'm flattered that you think I'm worth visiting. Or remembering."

To his surprise, Carmine leaned down and touched noses with him. "I didn't want to come this evening. Teek and Wisteria had to talk me into it. They were right, and I was wrong."

"If you can say that, you're already ahead of Arcove at your age," said Charder, and Carmine smiled again.

"I am sorry you will not be in Leeshwood this fall," continued the cat.

"So am I," said Charder. "I thought at first I might make the conference, but now I'm sure I won't. I..." It felt humiliating to ask twice, but... *I am dying.* "Can you tell Arcove I would like to see him?"

"We'll tell him," said Wisteria.

Charder woke late the next day, confused. He lay in the sun and had a long, rambling conversation with Pathar, who turned out to be So-fet when he came to himself around noon. "I'm sorry, my love."

"It's alright," she whispered, grooming his ears.

"I thought you were someone else."

"I know."

When he got up to take a drink and relieve himself, his heart raced so hard that he thought it would explode. He saw spots for a moment before he lay back down again.

Charder felt very cold that night, in spite of the mild weather. So-fet wrapped herself around him. He shivered still.

At dawn, she went out to forage. Charder was drifting in and out of dreams when he heard her say, "Well, you made him wait long enough."

Charder raised his head and saw Arcove's massive silhouette framed in dawn light. Charder tried to speak, coughed, tried again. "I didn't think you would come."

Arcove didn't answer at once. He seemed to waver in the entrance and Charder felt a stab of...what? Hurt feelings? *Surely I am beyond such things.* But he thought that perhaps he should not have insisted on this meeting. Clearly Arcove did not want to be here.

At last, the cat paced on into the cave, the dim light catching in his green eyes. He studied Charder, who supposed he must look like a shadow of himself—his spine prominent, the planes of his flanks sunken, his whole body smaller.

Then Arcove met his eyes and said, in an oddly formal voice, "Charder Ela-ferry, I have come as you requested. Do you...want me to do anything for you?"

Charder blinked. And suddenly he understood. Ferryshaft did not practice mercy killing. Not of their own kind. It was forbidden. But creasia did. Charder had seen Arcove do it more than once. *He thinks I want him to make an end of me. And he's dreading it.*

"Arcove," Charder's voice came out even softer than he'd intended. And then, because he was dying, because he had no inhibitions left, he said, "Dear friend, be at peace. I don't need you to kill me. I am dying quite comfortably. Just sit and talk to me a while. That's all I wanted."

Arcove shut his eyes and slowly sat down. He looked so relieved that Charder couldn't help teasing him a bit. "Although you did offer to kill me so many times in the past."

Arcove made a chuffing noise—creasia laughter, but he didn't look amused.

I should have known what you'd think when I sent you that message. Ghosts, I just told Carmine how you offered it to Coden.

Arcove still looked like he was gathering his wits, so Charder continued, "Last night, I had a wonderful conversation with your son and Teek and Wisteria. She calls you 'dear old Papa Arcy,' but don't tell her I said so. Why don't you spar with Carmine, Arcove? He would treasure it."

Arcove rolled his eyes at the bit about Wisteria and finally seemed goaded into speech. "Because if I beat him, he'll just keep trying, and if he beats me…"

Charder cocked his head. "If he beats you, what? He'll kill you? You won't be king anymore?"

Arcove's ears settled at an embarrassed angle.

I have gotten so much better at reading creasia faces, thought Charder with no small amount of smugness.

"I—"

"Are you afraid he'll learn your techniques and use them against you?" persisted Charder.

Arcove's tail lashed. "I don't know," he admitted. "Sparring with a potential challenger was not…done."

"Was," said Charder.

Arcove looked away.

"What if sometimes he wins and sometimes you win, and the outcome isn't as important as enjoying each other's company?"

"It would be nice to think it could be that way."

"It could."

Arcove's shoulders relaxed and he stretched out on his belly. "Is that your advice, councilor?"

"It is. Roup would agree with me."

"He would. He does."

"Good. He'll still be around to tell you this fall."

Arcove's expression fell again.

Charder watched him. *You are taking this harder than I expected.*

Arcove shook himself and spoke as though at random. "Twins?"

Charder beamed. "My grandfoals, yes. They are terribly mischievous. They'll come back soon and pester you with questions, I expect."

"I haven't seen many ferryshaft twins."

"On good grass, when females are not distressed, it happens."

Something like anxiety flashed through Arcove's eyes. Charder felt certain he was thinking of all the conversations they'd had about ways to keep the ferryshaft population within the parameters Arcove had set after the war—painful conversations, painful compromises. *Let's not talk about that. There's no need.*

Fortunately, the twins in question charged into the cave at that moment and provided a distraction. They tripped over each other at the sight of Arcove, creating a comical flurry of tails and legs. They ran out of the cave and ran back in again, this time trailed by their parents. Their combination of awe, nerves, curiosity, and delight was so transparent that even Arcove soon had his ears up and a smile tugging at the corner of his mouth.

The foals asked him questions about hunting sheep. Arcove had opinions about hunting sheep. They moved on to deer hunting, then fishing, then to Arcove's contribution in the Cave of Histories.

Arcove navigated all of these topics well enough. Finally they asked him about Leeshwood, and here Arcove became more circumspect.

"Grandpa Charder said we might go to Leeshwood this fall!" exclaimed Perdie, who was the more scatterbrained of the two. But he was perceptive enough to stop when he saw the adults' faces. "I mean— We—"

"I was going to take them to the fall conference," said Charder quickly. He hadn't planned for them to attend the actual meeting, of course, but it had become common for young animals of various species to mingle and visit when everyone gathered to assess the threat of the Volontaro. To the foals, Charder said, "I am afraid you will have to wait for Storm to arrange a visit to Leeshwood if he so chooses." He flashed a glance at Arcove and added, "If the many creasia whose territories you will be invading permit it."

Charder's daughter and her mate stayed for a while after the foals had dashed out again, but Charder could tell they were nervous in the presence of a creasia king, and Arcove was not volunteering to fill the silences. Soon they excused themselves, promising to return later.

The cave grew quiet. Charder was on the edge of dozing when Arcove said, "I never knew my father."

Charder blinked at him. He thought for a moment. "You knew him well enough to avenge him."

Arcove flicked his tail. "I avenged my brother and sister. I don't remember my father."

Charder struggled to make sense of this turn of the conversation. He gave up. "I may not be thinking clearly because I'm dying, but I'm not sure what you're—"

"I don't know what to do with Carmine," said Arcove, who'd clearly been mulling it over ever since Charder brought up the subject. "He's too much like me. It's easy with most of my offspring. It's *always* easy when they're cubs, and he was so bright and sharp, even when he was little. I think sometimes…in the natural order of things…he *should* beat me. Maybe he *should* kill me. I don't—"

"Arcove," interrupted Charder, and then wasn't sure how to continue.

Arcove had subsided, though. After a moment, he said, "You have a wonderful family. You make it look easy."

Oh. "It's not always easy," said Charder slowly. "I'm not sure I did a very good job the first time. Or the second. I've been incredibly lucky in the number of chances I've gotten."

"You lost mates and foals in the war," said Arcove. It wasn't a question. "Did I kill them?"

I will never get used to your bluntness. "Not directly." He hesitated. "It was a war, Arcove. It started before either of us were born. It was ugly and unfair and we don't have to revisit it." Charder found, to his annoyance, that he was shivering again. *Even in the daytime?*

Arcove looked suddenly abashed and said. "Is my scent making you uncomfortable? If I'm making this worse—"

"No," said Charder. "I'm just cold. Not enough flesh left on me, I suppose."

Arcove got up and came forward. "Would it be better or worse if I lay down beside you?"

Charder cocked his head. *You* are *treating me like a creasia. First you offer to kill me. Then you offer to curl up around me.* He almost laughed. *Cats.* Aloud, he said, "So-fet has been trying to keep me warm, but she deserves a chance to forage and stretch her legs. I suppose, if you want to…"

There was one moment, as Arcove came around behind him, when Charder *did* feel the bite of old instincts. Creasia scent and hot breath on his neck. *Run!* But then Arcove draped his head across Charder's shoulders, and he was as warm as sunbaked rock. *That really is better.* In a moment of ludicrous boldness, Charder said, "Creasia make a pleasant noise sometimes. Storm used to talk about Teek making it when he was little."

Arcove's voice was a rumble. "Noise?"

"A throbbing noise. I've only heard it a few times. I always thought it was a comforting sound."

A moment of confused silence, and then Arcove laughed. He raised his head and laughed until Charder craned his neck around to look at him. "Have I said something very foolish? I am dying, and so—"

"You want me to purr for you?"

Charder couldn't quite read his tone, except that he was amused. *Perhaps I should stop congratulating myself on how well I understand creasia.* "Do creasia not purr when they are content?"

Arcove rearranged himself—fitting the curve of his body to Charder's back. He slid one paw over Charder's front legs and under his chin. Once again, there was that fleeting sense of panic. *He's pinning me down...* But he was so warm. Arcove settled once again with his head across Charder's back and shoulders in a posture that Charder had seen countless times among den-mates and friends in Leeshwood. "Cubs purr in contentment," murmured Arcove, "at their mother's belly. Adults don't purr very often. Only in love, in pain, and in sorrow." Another pause. "I think I can manage it."

Charder didn't know what to say. *You are taking this much too hard.* "Arcove."

"Hmm?"

"You asked if I wanted you to do anything for me, and there is something."

Arcove's breathing stilled.

Charder couldn't see his face. "Take me to the Ghost Wood... when I'm gone."

The stillness continued for a beat. Then, instead of an answer, Charder heard a deep, low thrumming noise that seemed to fill the cavern and vibrate his whole body. He'd never been this close to a purring cat. After a moment, he rested his head on Arcove's paw that was across his front legs. "Ghosts and little fishes. Storm was right; that is pleasant."

Arcove spoke against his ear, still purring. "I will take you to the Ghost Wood, Charder Ela-ferry. And I will miss you."

Things that he might have said flickered through Charder's head, inadequate. "Thank you."

"But will your family be offended? Ferryshaft don't carry away tokens of their dead." Indeed, it was something Arcove had done during the war to inspire fear.

"I'll tell them," said Charder sleepily. The purring had somehow soothed the background nausea that had been his constant companion for the last few days. He shook his ears to wake himself and said, "You can talk and purr at the same time!"

"Not very well," muttered Arcove.

"You're like a telshee, singing in two voices. I can't believe I'm still learning things about cats on the day I die. Dying of old age, at that. Two things I thought I'd never do."

He thought Arcove said something, but Charder was already slipping off to sleep.

He floated to the surface sometime later. Arcove had moved, and So-fet was lying against him. Arcove was still purring, and they were talking over his head—low, friendly voices. Charder thought they were talking about Carmine and Wisteria and Teek. He wanted to add something, but he couldn't quite follow along. He thought, *It's the middle of the day, Arcove. Why are you awake?*

He managed to open his eyes and turn to catch So-fet's. "Arcove is going to take me to the Ghost Wood. I asked him to."

"I know," she said gently. "You told me."

"I'm sorry; I'm confused."

"It's alright, love. Everything is alright."

Arcove's purr resonated through his dreams. Charder was a young adult, running with his first herd over the plain. He was laughing at Pathar, poking at prickly things in tidepools. He was sparring with Coden on a spring day, amazed at his quick reactions, even as a juvenile. Coden was full of jokes and tricks and youthful vitality. *You never had to get old,* thought Charder. *You never had to live a long life with the memories and consequences of everything you'd ever done. You never had to meet the next generation or see your choices through their eyes. You were lucky in that way.*

Charder was in the cave again, and it was late afternoon. Arcove had switched places with So-fet. Charder could tell he was dozing, but still purring. Even in his sleep.

Storm and Tollee were standing near the mouth of the cave, talking to So-fet and a few other ferryshaft that Charder couldn't quite see in the brightness outside. When Storm noticed that Charder was awake, he came cautiously forward, shooting little glances at Arcove over the top of Charder's head. Charder wondered whether Storm was concerned that Arcove would startle awake and forget that they were friends. *He won't.*

"Charder?"

"Hmm?"

Storm smiled. "You're well-loved. I hope you know that."

Charder smiled back at him.

Arcove stirred at the sound of Storm's voice. "Storm," he said sleepily. "Is that Sauny I hear outside?"

Storm's tail waved. "It is. She has some news for you about the creasia in the Southern Mountains, but she didn't want to wake you."

"Tell her to come in."

Charder could feel an unnatural sleep pressing him down. *The final sleep?* Arcove's purr throbbed against his back. "Arcove..."

"Hmm?"

"It's not bad. Getting old."

A long sigh. "You make it look easy."

The cave was full of animals as evening deepened. They were saying interesting things, telling stories. Some of the stories were about Charder. He woke occasionally to laugh at a joke or listen to a recounting of some long-ago hunt.

Frogs sang. Arcove purred. Night fell.

Charder listened to his family and his friends.

He drifted in.

And out.

And in.

And out...

Part 2

I

Roup woke well ahead of his den-mates, as usual. He left Caraca cuddled up with two of her tame oories and padded past a grandcub, who'd come for a visit. Roup stepped lightly around Lyndi, sleeping in the entrance to the den, and out into the late afternoon sunshine. He stopped in surprise when he found Arcove curled up beneath the rock overhang, just out of sight of the cave's mouth.

He was sleeping, but woke instantly at Roup's approach. His third eyelid took a moment to slide out of sight as he blinked—evidence that he was tired. Roup couldn't imagine what had been important enough to bring Arcove to his den in the daytime, but not sufficiently important to wake anyone.

Before Roup could speak, Arcove said, "Charder is dead."

"Oh..." Roup sat down slowly. "I only just heard he was sick..."

Arcove said nothing.

Roup thought for a moment. "Did you get to say goodbye?"

"Yes."

Roup looked at him narrowly, trying to decide whether he should press for details.

"He asked me to take him to the Ghost Wood. I'll be gone for a few nights. I just wanted you to know."

Roup cocked his head. "Charder asked you to…?" He caught sight of a red fluff of tail lying on the ground. He felt a jolt—memories from the war. But this tail had not been taken in animosity. At least, Roup hoped not. "Does his mate know? What about the other ferryshaft? Charder had a lot of friends—"

Arcove looked impatient. "Yes, he told them. I'm going now. I just wanted you to know that you're in charge." Arcove bent to pick up the tail and started away.

"Wait." Roup trotted after him. "You're going to the Ghost Wood alone?"

Arcove had his mouth full and he didn't answer. He didn't slow down, either.

"Arcove, there have been reports of cats disappearing on the way to the Ghost Wood all summer. You heard from Halvery about it only last month, remember? And I had another den complaining two nights ago of a missing cat who'd taken a cub to the Ghost Wood."

Arcove slowed, although Roup could tell he didn't want to. He dropped Charder's tail and said, "The weather is pleasant. They probably stopped beside the lake to hunt and fish."

"That's what I said at first, but it's been over a month for some of them."

"Accidents happen. Curbs happen. I'm not some feckless four-year-old."

"I know." Roup looked hard at him. There was a dull stubbornness in those green eyes that he knew better than to argue with. Roup took a step back. "I'll see you in a few nights."

He waited until Arcove disappeared between the trees, then turned and trotted back to his den. He nudged Lyndi awake and said, "I'm going to be gone for a while. You're in charge of Leeshwood."

She blinked at him. "Wha...?"

"You're in charge," repeated Roup. "If you need help, ask Nadine. Although...she's been feeling poorly lately." Nadine was Charder's age, a fact that surely hadn't escaped Arcove. "Ask Caraca," said Roup with a twinkle. It was a joke. Caraca hated politicking.

Lyndi blinked sleep out of her eyes. "Alright... I assume you're going somewhere with Arcove. What about Halvery?" A reasonable question. He outranked her.

Roup turned away. "Halvery is coming with me."

"Does he know that?"

"Not yet."

II

It was midnight by the time Roup found Halvery. Fortunately, he was in the western part of his territory, trying to settle a den dispute. Under other circumstances, Roup would have tried to help, but not tonight. "Halvery, I need you to come with me to the Ghost Wood. It's urgent."

"What? Why?"

Roup stepped closer to him and spoke quietly. "Arcove went alone, and I don't think he should have. I'll explain on the way. Just come."

Around them, the circle of unhappy creasia continued a low-grade squabble. A pair of cubs were tussling on the ground, and the tension in the adults had brought out their claws. One scratched the other across the nose, and the loser fled, shrieking.

Halvery looked like he was being pulled in too many directions. "I'm trying to do something here!"

"I know. And I'll help you later. I'll manage it myself if you like. Please?"

Halvery stood still for a moment, flicking his short, third-of-a-tail. Then he rounded on his subordinates. "Alright, you lot, I have council-level problems to deal with. I will consider what you've told me and make a ruling in a few nights. If you start attacking each other, I will return and break up your dens. Do you understand?"

Unhappy growls all around. "What are we supposed to do with the ferryshaft in the meantime?" whined a juvenile male.

"Nothing!" snapped Halvery. "You will do nothing with them or to them, or I'll have your whiskers. If you start killing ferryshaft unprovoked, that's a treaty violation."

"But they're in our territory!"

"Not if they're on the trail."

"This wasn't a trail until recently!"

"I told you I would consider the problem. I'll be back in a few nights."

He stalked away with Roup, still bristling. "Overgrown cubs."

"Are ferryshaft really making new trails?" asked Roup in alarm.

The trails were a source of tension, but Roup hadn't heard of any recent hostilities. Laws surrounding these paths had sprung up in the first few years after the war, when ferryshaft incursions into Leeshwood had seemed poised to spark new violence. Cats were territorial to a degree that ferryshaft were not. It was difficult for ferryshaft to understand that a cat who had been friendly at a conference or during a chance meeting in the Great Cave might actually kill them if they wandered into a den or through prized hunting grounds unannounced and uninvited. Ferryshaft were curious by nature. As new generations grew up without the shadow of creasia raids, they fearlessly ventured into Leeshwood.

In addition, ferryshaft were ranging farther across the island than before. They needed to send messages between herds and were sometimes forced to pass through Leeshwood as a matter of course.

The problem had been solved by identifying a few well-established game trails for use as common ways. This had been Keesha's idea. He assured Arcove that it was done in other worlds—an idea that Arcove found not remotely reassuring. But the tactic had worked. As long as the ferryshaft stayed on the trails, the creasia tolerated their passage through the wood. However, creating new trails was not part of the arrangement.

"Did the den identify the ferryshaft in question?" asked Roup. "Whose herd were they from?"

Halvery matched Roup's flowing stride through the moonlit wood. "The ferryshaft aren't making new trails on purpose. The old trail ran near Martinique's den, and that group has never liked it. Recently, they got the bright idea of obliterating the trail and rerouting it through their neighbor's territory. Now those cats are upset."

Roup rolled his eyes. "Ghosts and little fishes."

"Overgrown cubs," repeated Halvery. "I'll sort it out in a few nights. I assume I won't be gone longer?"

"I don't think so. I don't know. Charder died, and Arcove took him to the Ghost Wood."

Halvery glanced at Roup as though to make sure he'd heard correctly. "Charder Ela-ferry?"

"Yes."

"Arcove took a ferryshaft to the Ghost Wood?"

"Yes."

"Why?"

Roup didn't try to answer this. They came out of the trees beside the Igby River and ran faster along open ground.

After a moment, Halvery said, "Why didn't you go with him?"

"He told me not to."

"So we are violating Arcove's direct orders. I see."

"*I* am. You're just doing what your superior officer told you to do."

"Why didn't you take Lyndi?"

"Because I want someone who can fight. She's good, but you're better."

Halvery tried to look as though he wasn't flattered and failed. "What am I supposed to be fighting?"

"I don't know. Cats have been disappearing while coming and going from the Ghost Wood all summer. You know that."

Halvery flicked his tail. "Maybe a dozen. Probably less. It's hardly a massacre, and Arcove can take care of hims—"

"Arcove is grieving and not thinking clearly. And he's alone."

Roup expected Halvery to sneer at the assertion that Arcove was grieving a ferryshaft and an old rival at that, but Halvery just looked a little baffled and went silent. They were moving fast enough to make conversation difficult, and they ran in silence for a while.

At last, Halvery said, "Aren't we going in the wrong direction?"

Most creasia traveling to the Ghost Wood followed the Igby River to Chelby Lake and then continued around its edge. Roup and Halvery were following the river back toward the cliffs. "I don't think he'll go the usual way," said Roup. "I could be wrong. We'll cross at a shallow spot and look for his trail."

Summer had been hot and the river was running low. It didn't take them long to find a crossing point, but Roup was right. There was no evidence that Arcove had come this way.

"You might have beaten him coming east," said Halvery doubtfully. "We might run straight into him. In that case, I hope you plan to do the talking."

Roup shook his head. "I don't think he'll come this way at all."

"You think he'll follow the cliffs? Why? It's so dry up there at this time of year."

"Because he doesn't want to run into anyone else. He wants to be alone."

"Oh…" Halvery considered. "Well, I don't understand any of this, but lead on, o sly one."

"Thank you," said Roup. *Thank you for not arguing with me and for not mocking what I said about Charder.*

The night was three-quarters spent when they picked up Arcove's trail in the boulders at the foot of the cliffs. "He's got most of a night's start on us," said Halvery.

"Yes, but he's tired. He looked like he'd been awake all day. I think we can catch up."

Tired or not, Arcove hadn't slowed down in the boulder mazes. Fortunately, he wasn't trying to hide his trail, either. He crossed the Igby at its headwaters and kept going north, skirting the grass plains, where the ferryshaft had lived after the war. Here Arcove had slackened his pace a little. He'd lingered for some time in a clearing among the boulders where Roup knew he and Charder had used to meet.

The scent trail grew fresher. At last, Halvery said, "Roup, are we trying to catch up with him in order to have a conversation? Do you know what you're going to say? Because I'm not sure we can get close to him undetected. He may not be quite himself, but he's still…Arcove."

Roup sighed and stopped walking.

"Also," said Halvery in an annoyingly patient voice, "he will smell us on his way back. Unless he returns via the lake. He'll know we followed him, even if we manage to stay out of sight."

Roup hadn't thought that far ahead. He flicked his tail, thinking. "He wants to do this alone. Maybe he needs to. I'm not trying to stop him. I just want to make sure he's alright."

"We could climb the cliff," offered Halvery. "Follow him from there."

Roup's eyes tracked up the red rock, clearly visible in the light of a full, golden moon. *Hunter's moon. Let's hope it's your luck tonight, Arcove.* Aloud, he said, "We couldn't help him if he got into trouble."

"Yes, but as you've pointed out, he's not going to the Ghost Wood via the usual route. The cats who disappeared went by Chelby Lake, so whatever happened to them happened over there. Maybe he's safe going this way. If he does cross the plain, we'll have time to come down and catch up with him. I doubt he'll run. He doesn't think he's being chased. If he returns via the cliffs, our scent may have dissipated by the time he reaches this area. At least we won't be laying down a fresh trail right behind him."

Sound reasoning. "Alright," said Roup aloud, "you win. Let's climb."

"Now you're just humoring me."

"No, I'm serious; it's a good idea. But we'll lose time in the ascent. Let's go."

Roup had a vivid memory of hunting Storm along this exact cliff trail. It seemed thoroughly ironic to be out here hunting Arcove.

Up and up, and the island unfurled beneath them in the brightening dawn—red rock directly below, fading into green and brown grasses, tall at this time of year, and dotted with scrubby trees, stretching away to the distant woods and sparkle of Chelby Lake. Behind them, the silver line of the Igby marked the edge of the darker shadows of Leeshwood. Farther away, to the north, lay the more uniform darkness of the Ghost Wood at the edge of the plain.

"There," said Halvery, when they were about halfway to the top.

Roup looked and spotted Arcove's dark silhouette wending between the boulders, moving steadily north. "He's not acting like he's been awake all day," muttered Halvery.

Birds were singing by the time they topped the cliff beside the little belt of trees on the ridge. Roup had managed to keep an eye on Arcove throughout the climb, though he was nearly out of sight now. They pushed for speed along the clifftop.

Halvery had been right. Arcove was moving swiftly, but not like a hunted animal. They *could* overtake him if they needed to.

Roup was feeling the beginnings of strain from traveling all night and into the day. He was sure Halvery felt it, too, although neither one of them said anything as they caught up to Arcove and continued to follow him at a more leisurely pace from the top of the cliff. *He really may not stop at all.* "Halvery, if you want to sleep, you can probably catch up. I'll just—"

"Don't patronize me," growled Halvery. "I'm fine."

Roup hardly heard him. Half to himself, he muttered, "I hope Charder didn't ask him to end it." He hadn't gotten that impression from the way Arcove was behaving, but—

Halvery cut into his thoughts, "Would Arcove have found that difficult?"

Roup bit his tongue on what he wanted to say. "Yes."

"Why?"

Don't, thought Roup. *Don't talk about this to Halvery.* But he was tired and worried, and Halvery had followed him all the way out here with very little complaining and no real explanation. *I should try to explain about Charder.* Instead, he said, "Arcove never talks about Ariand. I wish he had come with me to take him to the Ghost Wood."

Halvery frowned. "Why didn't he?"

Roup looked away. "He said, 'He asked you.'"

Halvery cocked his head. "Ariand asked Arcove to kill him… but he asked you to take him to the Ghost Wood?"

"Yes," said Roup. Halvery hadn't been there. He'd been running for his life from Treace's cats at the time.

"I'm sure Ariand didn't mean anything by it," began Halvery.

"Of course he didn't," said Roup. "He was in terrible pain. He was dying. But I wish—"

"I'd probably say the same thing in his place."

Roup gave a tired bark of laughter. "You certainly would not!"

"Well, not at that time, but now."

"Why?"

"Because…" Halvery seemed to struggle for the moment.

"Yes, I'm the soft one," said Roup acidly.

"You're the sweet one," said Halvery with something between fondness and malice.

"Well, I'm telling you right now that if you ever ask Arcove to put you down, *please* also ask him to take you to the Ghost Wood!"

Roup turned to emphasize his point with a glare, and Halvery missed a step. "Alright," he said meekly.

Roup knew he was overreacting. *Come on, Arcove, stop for a rest. Before I bite Halvery's head off.* Against his better judgment, he said, "When he'd fight and kill a challenger…usually the cat had family and friends to take them to the Ghost Wood. But if he didn't… Arcove would do it. Even before he was king."

Halvery was silent for a moment. "I didn't know that."

"He took Treace," whispered Roup, and then he stopped walking. *I shouldn't have said that.* "He doesn't know I followed him. No one knows. Please don't—"

"Roup." Halvery sounded surprised, but steady.

Roup raised his eyes.

"Thank you for trusting me."

Roup let out his breath. "Arcove has taken a lot of animals to the Ghost Wood. I don't like it when he goes alone, but this isn't the first time. I've dragged you on what is probably a fool's errand."

"Well, I haven't seen you do many foolish things, but if this turns out to be one of them, I would be sorry to miss it."

Roup laughed. To his embarrassment, Halvery leaned over and started grooming his ears. "I'm on your side."

"Thank you."

"Is that why he's taking Charder? The way he'd take an old rival? To quiet the ghost?"

"No..." Roup shook Halvery off and resumed following Arcove along the cliff. "Charder and Arcove were friends."

Halvery looked like he was sincerely trying to understand and failing. "I knew they were friend*ly* at conferences and such, but Charder grew up going on raids and killing cubs. Ferryshaft *ate* cubs, Roup! They almost ate *you!* And then Charder surrendered to Arcove without a fight at the end of the war. If there's one thing Arcove does not respect, it's cowardice. How could he ever become friends with—?"

"At first, he didn't," interrupted Roup. "Although it wasn't the surrender that predisposed Arcove to hate Charder. It was me. Because I got hurt in Charder's herd."

Halvery said nothing. He'd heard Roup tell the story of his cubhood, but they'd never spoken about it since.

"Arcove punished him for that. He's always been inclined to hold my grudges." Half under his breath, Roup muttered, "He holds them longer than I do."

Halvery laughed. "That's one way of putting it."

Roup took a deep breath. "Charder just...took it...with as much dignity and grace as he could manage. Immediately after the war, there was a real danger that the ferryshaft would break their treaty agreements. Then Arcove would have felt compelled to annihilate them, because he wouldn't have been able to trust them to keep their word. They out-breed us so quickly… They would have been right back to raiding and killing cubs in no time unless Arcove thoroughly broke the cycle with future generations. We were in a precarious place until some ferryshaft grew up who didn't remember doing that.

"All of the adults in Charder's herd remembered being masters of Lidian. They remembered how to kill us. Charder had to deal with all that injured pride and sullen resentment, directed at himself as much as anyone else.

"He had to be the liaison between Arcove and the herd elders. He had to figure out how to keep ferryshaft numbers within parameters. He tried to do it with breeding restrictions. That didn't work. The herd elders agreed on the cull, because they knew that they were unlikely to be taken. Charder hated the cull. Arcove didn't like it, either. But a random cull was the only thing that worked.

"Charder was despised by his own kind for a long time. He had to make decisions, knowing that no matter what he chose, someone would suffer. He had to do this with very little in the way of support. You don't get much sympathy when you're the one making the choices that get someone's foal killed."

Halvery was being very quiet. Roup thought he was beginning to understand.

"When did Arcove stop hating him?"

"I don't know. Long before Storm. But he couldn't show it. If he was soft on ferryshaft, even a little, he thought they'd take advantage. He thought his control of Leeshwood might slip. He thought there would be another war and even more animals would die. He couldn't show Charder compassion without risking everything he'd fought for. And I suppose Charder didn't feel like he could give anything away, either, when dealing with Arcove. They couldn't be friends...or even friendly. But they both grew to respect each other. And after the rebellion was over, after all that pressure was gone..."

"I understand," said Halvery quietly. "Thank you for explaining."

Roup was aware of exhaustion loosening his tongue. *Well, you always wanted to be part of the inner circle, Halvery. Is this what you had in mind?* "Charder and I were friend*ly* as you say. But not friends. I bore him no ill will, but...growing up in his herd was hard. He wasn't *my* friend. He was Arcove's."

"Do you think that's why Arcove doesn't want you along?"

"Maybe."

Halvery thought for a moment. "You and Ariand were better friends than Arcove and Ariand."

"Yes."

"That's why Ariand asked you to take him to the Ghost Wood, Roup. If he'd asked you to kill him, too, could you have done it?"

Roup stopped walking. He wasn't conscious of his expression, but Halvery was suddenly grooming his ears again. "Alright, stop thinking about that. You really are the sweet one. I'm sorry I said it. I mean it; stop thinking about it, Roup. We're not all good at the same things."

"Arcove can end a friend's suffering," whispered Roup. "He can be the last thing you ever see, the last thing you ever hear. And he can make it look natural and easy, but it's not."

"I know," said Halvery. "I've had to put a few of mine down. It's always awful." He hesitated. "But you don't think Charder asked him for that?"

"I don't think so. I could be wrong."

Halvery made a face. "Why ask Arcove to take him to the Ghost Wood at all? Ferryshaft don't do that. They think it's perverse to bite off tails and ears and such from a dead friend."

Roup smiled sadly. "Isn't it obvious? Charder knew Arcove would need to mourn him…in the way that creasia mourn."

A long silence. At last, Halvery shook himself. "You make the world easier to understand, Roup. I suppose that's why you're his beta. I should borrow your expertise about a problem I'm having, but right now I'm very tired, so it may come out wrong."

The sun was halfway up the sky. Arcove was still moving through the boulders below.

"I feel like staying awake all day used to be easier," grumbled Halvery.

"It did," said Roup. "We're getting old."

"Ugh. How did that happen? Alpha creasia don't get old."

"They never have before, and that's part of what's bothering Arcove, as well. He's slowing down."

"He is not!" said Halvery indignantly.

"He is," said Roup. "He's as quick as he ever was at the beginning of a fight, but he gets tired faster than he used to. Carmine is in my clutter, and you only have to watch him spar to remember what Arcove was like at twelve. There *is* a difference. He's forty-one, Halvery! And Nadine is Charder's age, and she won't be with us much longer. Watching Charder get old and die reminded Arcove that others will, too. That *he* will. Or he may. And that scares him. I just hope that Charder...showed him how it's done. Because I *really* want him to get old." Roup knew he was letting an unacceptable level of emotion into his voice. *This is not how you talk to a subordinate, and Halvery is so very attached to the chain of command.*

But Halvery only said, "I think he will if you will."

"He could live another ten, even twenty years," whispered Roup, "but he won't be able to kill everything in his path. That time is coming to an end. It will be a difficult transition."

"Is Carmine going to challenge him?"

"I don't think so. Carmine is a good cub."

"Carmine should challenge Hollygold or Stefen...or Moashi." Halvery gave a derisive snort. "He should definitely challenge Moashi." These were creasia who'd taken over territory previously belonging to Ariand, Treace, and Sharmel. They were the lowest ranking members of the creasia council, junior to Roup, Halvery, and Lyndi.

Roup rolled his eyes. "Because Moashi is so popular with all the den mothers?"

"Because he didn't fight for his clutter!" exploded Halvery. "Sharmel died, and Moashi just walked in and made himself cozy. And because he's charming and pretty, nobody shredded his ears for him."

Roup's laugh echoed among the trees. "You're one to talk. I know how *you'll* avoid getting old if you're not careful."

Halvery looked uncomfortable. "About that..." He glanced over the cliff and interrupted himself. "Thank all the peaceful ghosts! He's stopped."

Roup came to the edge and stared for a long moment. Arcove had settled down atop a flat rock in the sun. It was near noon. "I wish he would pick somewhere more sheltered to sleep."

"Why? It's pleasant in the sun and there's no one else out here. Even ferryshaft aren't daft enough to hang about in these dry boulders in the summertime."

Roup took another long look. Nothing moved in the wavering heat. "You're right."

"He'll reach the Ghost Wood easily tonight," said Halvery. "We're over halfway there."

Roup relaxed and sat down. He yawned.

"Can we go under the trees to sleep?" asked Halvery. "Or do you have to shut your eyes within sight of him?"

Roup gave a tired smile. "We can go under the trees." Sleeping on the edge of the cliff would be stupidly dangerous.

Halvery didn't go far, though. He was clearly tired, and he curled up in the leaves without spending much time looking for a good spot. After an instant's hesitation, Roup lay down nose to tail with him. He draped his head across Halvery's flanks, much as he would have done with Arcove. Halvery grunted and shifted to put his own head over Roup's back. Creasia found this sort of contact comforting when they were far from their home territory.

In spite of his extreme weariness, Roup did not fall asleep at once. Nothing smelled familiar, and he kept thinking about Arcove sleeping alone in the open.

Halvery kept fidgeting, too. "How do you know he's slowing down?" he muttered at last. "Does he spar with you? I haven't seen him fight in a while."

"He spars with me," mumbled Roup.

"How often?"

Roup tried to repress an absurd sense of embarrassment. "Pretty often…"

"I've never seen it."

Ghosts, Halvery. "Well, those matches usually end in a particular way, and we tend to avoid an audience."

To Halvery's credit, it only took him a beat. Then he laughed and kept laughing helplessly for a moment.

Roup contemplated getting up and finding somewhere else to sleep.

Halvery seemed to sense this and tucked his nose against Roup's flank in a gesture more common among littermates. "Oh, Roup, don't bristle at me. I'm sorry. You didn't have to tell me."

"I know that," snapped Roup. *I am tired and worried and saying too much.*

"It's just... *Of course,* that's Arcove's style! Of course it is." Halvery got up, turned around, and lay down again, so that their heads were pointed in the same direction. He licked Roup's ears until Roup stopped bristling, put his head down, and allowed himself to be groomed. "So, you spar with him," said Halvery. "Which means you legitimately know how he's doing. That's valuable."

"He could still take any of us," muttered Roup. "But I can see... the beginning of..."

He didn't finish the sentence.

Halvery yawned. He stopped grooming and put his head down beside Roup's. "You've shared your business; shall I share mine?"

Roup felt silly for bristling. "I know I sometimes ask a lot without an explanation."

"You do. But you've saved my life a few times. Always without an explanation."

Roup laughed. "I assume you were trying to tell me something about Ilsa. And you surely already know I'm going say that was a mistake, and you should send her away at once."

Halvery raised his head and said primly, "It is not my fault that pretty little six-year-olds want me to sire their cubs, Roup."

Roup made a grumbling noise. "She's *six?* I thought she was ten! So I assume this is her first den? Blood and gristle, Halvery. I want *you* to get old, too."

Halvery sighed. "I don't usually take six-year-olds, but she was very persuasive."

Roup rolled his eyes. "I'll bet. Halvery, you're a war hero. You're a high-ranking council member. You're charming, and you smell nice. Of course six-year-olds will show up at your den, but if you take them, you'll get ten and twelve-year-old-challengers, and you are forty-one, too!"

"Aw, Roup...I think I heard a compliment somewhere in there."

"Send her away."

"I smell nice?"

"She'll be in her prime when you're Charder's age, ever think of that? If someone doesn't kill you over her this year, they'll do it in five years or ten."

"And she can go somewhere else in five years or ten. I won't stop her." He gave Roup a nudge in the shoulder. "Six-year-olds would line up at your den, too, if you'd let them."

"They do. I send them away."

Halvery leaned against him good-naturedly. "Isn't Caraca done having cubs? And Lyndi can't. Come on, Roup, the world needs more of that golden fur."

"The world has an adequate number of my offspring. I think Wisteria all by herself is enough."

Halvery grinned at him. "*I* smell nice. You're *beautiful*. I don't know why any six-year-old in Leeshwood wouldn't want to have our cubs!"

Roup's ears were prickling. He forced them not to go flat with embarrassment. "Beautiful? Really?"

"Oh, don't be modest. You've got to know it's why you're alive. The ferryshaft went on a raid, brought back cubs to eat, and said, 'That one's too pretty to kill. Let's keep him and see what happens.'"

Roup choked on a laugh. "Halvery—"

"Then you wandered into Leeshwood a few years later, talking like a ferryshaft, *thinking* like a ferryshaft—frankly you still do— and picked a fight with the first cub you ran into—"

"I did *not* pick that fight."

"—who *happened* to be Arcove on the worst day of his life. But did he kill you? No. Because it would be a shame to put blood on that coat."

"Oh, he put blood on it, believe me."

"Well, he doesn't anymore. In spite of *frequent* opportunities."

Roup didn't know whether to laugh or bristle. He put his chin on the ground and spoke with heavy sarcasm. "The story of my life from your point of view is fascinating."

"You're too perceptive not to know this."

"You asked me about Ilsa, but you already know what I think, and you don't care. Was there something else?"

Halvery's bravado faded. "Well...I did think Kuno was going to challenge me over her."

"I don't know him," said Roup.

"A new den alpha in my clutter. He's fifteen."

Roup winced. "Watch yourself. He'll be quick, but he might not—"

"I'm not finished. Please stop getting ahead of me."

"I'm sorry. Continue."

"My whole clutter has been a bit…tense about this fight. Everyone knew it was going to happen. They just didn't know when. I suppose some of them were worried for me."

"I'm sure they were."

"Anyway…two nights ago, I was down by the lake, fishing with the cubs."

Roup couldn't help asking, "How many cubs?"

"Oh, fifteen or so." Halvery paused and nudged him again. "Stop laughing at me. I've got seven breeding females in my den."

"And one of them is six years old."

"She hasn't had a litter yet!"

"So you and a small army of cubs were down by the lake. Then what?"

"Nothing. We came back at dawn, carrying fish. Everyone was happy. My mates and cubs were eating and gossiping. But…I could tell something wasn't quite right. I cornered one of the juveniles who hadn't gone to the lake and after a lot of prevaricating, she told me that Kuno had come looking for me while I was gone, and the whole den had…driven him off. They told him that if he came back, they would kill him."

Roup raised his head to look at Halvery, who was not meeting his eyes. "Well…that's something different." He thought for a moment. "They love you dearly."

"I know," muttered Halvery. "I couldn't bear to punish them for it. But if word gets around that females are doing my fighting for me, I really will be in trouble. I'll have no end of challengers—not just for Ilsa, but for my whole clutter, for my place on the council. I don't know what to do about it."

Roup leaned over and started grooming his ears.

Halvery didn't raise his head. "You're going to say that I brought this on myself. Can we skip that part?"

"I'm going to say that your den is a happy place, and you inspire a great deal of love and loyalty."

"And *then* you're going to tell me I've gotten myself into a muddle."

"Well, yes."

Halvery squirmed. "Maybe I should just go find Kuno myself and get it over with."

"You might lose," said Roup. "Your mates think so, or they wouldn't have interfered."

He thought Halvery was going to dispute this, but he didn't. *You think so, too.*

Halvery started to say something, but Roup caught him gently behind the head and pushed his chin back down. "Quiet. I'm thinking." After a moment, he said, "Alright, I know how you spin it. This was about Ilsa's right to choose her den. Females have a right to

118

choose their mates. That idea has been gaining traction for the last decade. What happened at your den had *nothing* to do with you or your ability to fight. It was entirely about Ilsa and her clearly stated choice of mates. Kuno tried to force her to go with him. The den drove him off. End of story."

Halvery raised his head and blinked at Roup. He started to say something, stopped.

Roup tried to repress a smile. *No comment? I really did give you something to chew on.*

At last, Halvery said, "Did I mention that you are also very clever? In addition to the coat thing."

"No, but that's the *actual* reason I'm still alive. You're the only one who thinks I'm pretty."

"*Everyone* thinks you're pretty."

"I'm right, aren't I? That will work."

"I believe it will." Halvery was clearly still mulling it over. "I think… Yes, I do believe that angle may save my reputation and prevent me from fighting a string of young challengers. Although I'll have to make sure the rumor spreads properly."

"Velta can manage that." She was Halvery's alpha den mother, well past her breeding years, and chatty with other dens.

Halvery smiled. He draped his head over Roup's shoulders and relaxed. "Thank you, sir. I believe I can sleep now."

"You're welcome." Roup shut his eyes. "No more six-year-olds, please? Get old with us, Halvery."

A muted laugh. "I'll do my best."

III

Arcove woke at sunset. He'd expected to feel better after a little sleep, but he didn't. He felt as though he'd swallowed a river stone, and it sat cold and heavy in his belly. He was thirsty. He'd taken a long drink at the Igby, but had encountered no water since. He'd known it would be dry coming this way. *I'll cross the plain and drink at Chelby Lake. After I've done what I need to do.*

He turned to pick up Charder's tail.

It was gone.

Arcove sat bolt upright and looked around. He'd gone to sleep with the token under his chin and one paw. He hadn't moved much. If the tail had rolled or blown away, it shouldn't have gone far.

He froze. A curb was sitting perfectly still among the rocks below, watching him. The horrible little animal had Charder's tail between its jaws.

Arcove forced himself not to leap at it immediately. Curbs never traveled alone. His eyes skipped around the boulders, but he didn't see the rest of the pack. Finally, he spotted a second curb in the shadow of a rock. Try as he might, he couldn't see any others. The two of them were watching him closely, as though they expected him to do something specific.

Arcove remembered Roup's warning about traveling to the Ghost Wood alone. He remembered his own dismissal.

Arcove growled. He wasn't in the mood to be wrong about something this evening. He shot down from the rock, and the curbs bolted in the direction of the grass plains. "You'll want to give that back!" he thundered. "It's not worth what I'm going to do when I catch you!"

No words answered him, only quavering yips. The rest of the pack seemed to be farther out, scattered across the plain. *Why are they provoking me in this way?*

They were lowland curbs, and none of that species had been friendly to Leeshwood since Treace's rebellion. They'd chosen the wrong side and were still smarting over it. Arcove had ordered them killed on sight if they entered creasia territory. *But they can't have known I would be out here. I came straight from Charder's cave, and I didn't tell anyone apart from Roup.*

An unfamiliar, panicky sensation squeezed his chest. *I said I would take Charder to the Ghost Wood. I promised.*

Arcove wanted the tail back. He wanted it back *right now.*

At the same time, he was aware of a lack of clarity in his thinking—a vague sense of nausea, that relentless heaviness in the pit of his stomach, thirst, lack of sleep, the strain of purring all day and all night… *Don't think about that.*

The curbs were out of sight in the long grass, but Arcove was close enough to follow them by scent without slowing. He put on a burst of speed and reached the one who had Charder's tail.

Except, it didn't. The animal veered away, and Arcove saw that its jaws were empty. He *wanted* to catch up and rip the curb to pieces. He *needed* to find Charder's tail.

Arcove slowed, thinking the curb must have dropped it, but then a yip brought his attention back to the plain. Another curb had reared up above the grass. Charder's red fluff of tail whipped in the wind between its jaws.

They are leading me somewhere. This is not good.

But he tore after them. The pack was large, and they used their numbers to maximum advantage. They would pass off Charder's tail when they were out of sight among the grass. Whenever Arcove was close to catching one, another would pop up and wave the tail to get his attention.

Some part of Arcove's brain whispered that he was doing what an enemy expected, and this was never a wise decision. Another part said that he could not possibly be outrun by a pack of curbs. If he just pushed hard enough, he would catch them. He would bring Charder's tail to the Ghost Wood well before dawn, then travel to the lake for a drink and some sleep. Then he would return to hunt down every member of this miserable pack.

"I am going to have all your tails as den trophies!" he spat when he got close enough to the one that he thought was the leader. She was a little bigger than the others and seemed to initiate most of the yipping. She almost never carried the tail herself, which made him think she needed her mouth for signaling.

She spoke for the first time, her voice mocking, disappearing into the wind as she ran. "Arcove Ela-creasia... Can it really be? Come out all alone to our little stretch of Lidian? This is not a creasia tail you carry. Why is it so important to you?"

They all started calling to him, then, from many directions.

"So important."

"So special."

"Worth a long run."

"Worth dying."

"Creasia king, you're not so scary now."

"Not as big as I remember."

"No friends here, no ferryshaft, no highland curbs, no nasty sea snakes."

"Old cat, slow cat. What are you doing so far from home, cat?"

Arcove snarled. "You are all going to die if you don't give that back to me."

He thought he saw where they were leading him—to a little copse of trees on a rise. *Are even more curbs waiting there to attack me? What do they gain from this?*

He nearly tripped over something in the long grass. Arcove didn't slow down, and he got only a glimpse in the moonlight, but his nose told him the story: a dead creasia, decaying quickly in the summer heat.

Arcove's instincts were clamoring now. *Turn around and go back to the cliffs. Something that can kill creasia is out here. You are walking straight into a trap. This is an absurd way for a creasia king to die.*

But then a curb reared on its hind legs just a little ways down the hill from the copse of trees. It flung Charder's tail into the air with an exaggerated motion and pranced away. Arcove forced himself to slow as he approached the spot where the tail had landed.

Have they laid a vine trap? He'd stepped into one of those before and did not wish to do so again. But the spot where the tail had fallen was open ground, and curbs needed trees to make their traps deadly. *Something new?*

But no. There was nothing new here after all.

As Arcove neared the copse, ferryshaft began stealing out of the trees and down the hill towards him. At first there were three, and then there were eight, and then Arcove lost count. He had a guess now as to who they were.

Turn around, his instincts screamed. *Run while you've still got a lead. There are far too many of them.*

Arcove ignored his instincts. It was easy to do with that cold rock still sitting in his stomach and the memory of Charder's head on his paw. He glided over the last stretch of grass and snatched up the tail. By then, the ferryshaft were fanning out to surround him, the curbs, too, and he could see the whites of their leader's eyes.

Sedaron. He was Kelsy's father and contemporary with Charder. He looked grayer around the muzzle than the last time Arcove had seen him, but not frail.

Sedaron had disapproved of Charder's decision to help Arcove's creasia during Treace's rebellion. He'd left the conflict before its conclusion and led a likeminded group all the way around the island, to the far side of the Ghost Wood, where nobody had heard much from them since. They were rumored to be the largest ferryshaft herd currently on Lidian, and they included many of the elders from before the war.

Sedaron had been killing creasia before Arcove was born. Arcove was sure he'd trained the group now spreading out around him. It had been ten years since Treace's rebellion, and some of these ferryshaft had reached adulthood without ever having seen a raid. They had no fear of cats.

Sedaron's bright eyes gleamed in the moonlight as he stared at Arcove. "I thought the curbs were lying about who they'd found," he whispered. "I thought they were trying to impress me with absurd stories, but no… Our ancestors smile on us tonight. I have dreamed of this day. Arcove Ela-creasia alone here at my mercy…in the act of desecrating some ferryshaft's corpse! Is that Charder's tail? It looks like his fur. Did you finally murder him? Well, he was half a cat, so it hardly matters, but the irony…"

Arcove was seeing red. He was angry enough to drop the tail, putting one paw on it as he did so. "Have you been killing creasia who come to the Ghost Wood in mourning? That is despicable, Sedaron. Even by your very low standards."

Sedaron gave a snort and glanced at one of the ferryshaft beside him. "I forget they can talk sometimes. What with their mouths being full so often. Someone shut him up."

A curb dashed forward and made a grab for the tail. Arcove snatched it. Only then did he grasp the cruel genius of Sedaron's new method of hunting creasia. Arcove couldn't open his mouth without dropping the token of his dead friend. The irrational desire to cling to it was very strong. He imagined creasia with tokens from dead mates, dead cubs, dead companions—torn apart because they would not—could not—betray the final request of a dying friend.

I still have my claws... But the ferryshaft and curbs were beginning to circle, and Arcove knew how this would end. A group of ferryshaft with extensive experience killing cats were nearly impossible for a lone creasia to handle. They could work a cat for half the night, tiring him out, while using their greater numbers to rest and stay fresh. An attacker would always be rushing in on the cat's exposed back or flank. Eventually, they would sever a tendon or open a major blood vessel. Then the cat would be lame or bleeding, and they could kill him at their leisure.

If he'd been able to use his teeth, Arcove could have at least killed some of them and perhaps frightened the rest into retreat. Arcove could deliver a deadly, crushing bite in the blink of an eye. Claws, however, were more likely to land glancing blows under these circumstances. Without his teeth, he was far less dangerous.

The ferryshaft knew it. They were beginning their deadly dance almost lazily, nipping at him and leaping away, laughing.

Sedaron let the younger ones do the fighting. He stood back and watched. "This is how creasia should die," he murmured, "mute and flailing. The whole island is going to know what we did. We will take Arcove Ela-creasia to pieces, just as he did to ferryshaft during the war. We will send these trophies to every herd. Oh, but take your time, my friends. There is no hurry. I'd like to see him lame before he dies. I'd like to see him crawling."

If only I could put my back to something, thought Arcove. But he didn't trust the trees, where the ferryshaft had been hiding, and there was no other cover for a great distance.

Drop the tail and use your teeth, he told himself. *What good will it do Charder if you die here? He would tell you to drop it!*

Arcove did not drop it. He could hear his own heartbeat rushing in his ears. *Think. You've made several mistakes. One more and you're done.*

You have already made the fatal mistake, whispered a voice in his head. *It is too late.*

Arcove risked another glance at the copse of trees. Something about it looked familiar. He remembered chasing Storm across this plain to the edge of the Ghost Wood twelve years ago. Arcove had given him some hard choices, and Storm had had the temerity to ask, "What would you do, Arcove?"

Arcove remembered his reply as though it had been yesterday. *"I would fight and die. It is not in my nature to submit or to run away."*

He'd revised that stance during Treace's rebellion. And now... *I am taking Charder to the Ghost Wood if it is the last thing I do. I do not care what they think of me or whether I have to run away.*

What would Storm do?

And then he remembered.

Arcove made a feint at one of the circling ferryshaft, spun away, and leapt as high and as far as he could. He cleared the edge of their circle and hit the ground running.

The ferryshaft were not completely unprepared for this. Arcove certainly wasn't the first creasia to flee from impossible odds. Still, he'd struck out south, and that did seem to surprise them. They obviously expected him to run towards the Ghost Wood, towards the lake, or back towards the cliffs. There was no cover to the south for a long way—just wide open plain.

Except it's not as wide open as it looks. Hadn't Storm demonstrated that over and over again? Arcove had become acquainted with the dips and hollows of these fields while preparing for those hunts. It had been many years since he'd had to use that knowledge, but the memories came back. *There is an east-west trench just a little south of here. I should be beyond sight of the ferryshaft…right… about…now.*

The moment he judged he was below the level of the grass, Arcove changed directions, heading for the lake. Behind him, the ferryshafts' jokes and laughter changed to cries of alarm and confusion.

They've lost sight of me, so they can't cut me off. They'll see me again soon, but I'll have gained ground. And there's another low place coming up on my left.

He was shaking. That was irritating. Feelings for which he had no name sloshed around inside him. He realized that he was about to bite Charder's tail in half and forced his jaws to relax.

Ten years ago, Arcove would have been dreaming of ways to punish his tormentors. Ten years ago, he would have been looking for a spot to turn and make a stand.

Ten years ago, he would never have been out here alone, taking a ferryshaft to the Ghost Wood.

Arcove wondered whether he had lived too long. He wondered whether Carmine should have killed him some time ago. The image of Charder's head resting on his paw flickered through his brain and he felt that weight again, a sense that nothing mattered.

Behind him, the ferryshaft had figured out his trick. They were howling, signaling to each other, fanning out to try to prevent him from changing directions once more. Curbs yipped from much too close.

I can outrun them, thought Arcove.

Can you? asked a voice inside him. He was exhausted. They were not. He was thirsty. They were not. They were young—at least, some of them were—and he was not.

Don't think, he told himself. *Just run.*

IV

Keesha floated in the clear waters of Chelby Lake, examining the body of a creasia on the bottom. He thought that it had once been a lishty, although he could not be certain. Four-legged lishties were still turning up from time to time ever since Moro's experiments. Keesha had asked to be notified whenever one was found. Then he either went himself to deal with it, or he dispatched experienced telshees.

No one wanted land-based lishties. The idea of that strange intelligence gaining a permanent foothold in a new species was troubling to telshees, creasia, and ferryshaft alike. Keesha, however, still had hopes of completely eliminating the problem.

On the positive side, lishties didn't perform as well on four legs. They sometimes seemed to forget how to operate their hosts, and they often forgot that four-legged hosts did not last long at the bottom of a lake or river. Still, every time Keesha thought he'd destroyed the last of them, another one or two showed up. *There must be a reservoir of infection somewhere. I wish I could find it.*

Lishties still turned up most frequently around Kuwee Island, although Keesha wasn't certain whether animals were actually infected nearby or whether they were drawn there for some reason after infection. He'd taken to making an occasional sweep of the island and sometimes the shoreline of the lake, where drowned four-legged lishties occasionally washed up.

This particular one had washed nearly to Groth. Keesha worried anytime he found a lishty in that vicinity. He still thought that the carnivorous forest might wake and prove malevolent. He did not want those plants exposed to lishties or acriss. Keesha didn't think any of Moro's infected plants had survived or made it back into the established population, but he didn't want to take chances. He circled the creasia's decomposing body until he was satisfied that nothing glowed or moved in the corpse.

Foggy dawn was breaking as Keesha surfaced. Mist hung thick over the water, so that he could not see the shoreline. As he cleared his ears, Keesha was surprised to hear a commotion—curbs yipping and ferryshaft howls.

He listened with interest as the sounds drew nearer. Then something splashed into the lake, hidden by the sliding fog. Keesha heard the unmistakable noises of a land animal swimming towards him. It was making a strangled panting noise and an amount of splashing that seemed sloppy to a telshee.

Keesha dipped beneath the surface. To his eyes, the world beneath was clear in all directions, even in the gray dawn. Now he saw the swimmer—a cat, its dark legs cutting through the water from the direction of the shore. Tendrils of blood drifted down around it.

You seem to have made a lot of ferryshaft very angry. I wonder why?

Keesha watched as the cat continued to swim further out into the lake. The water was lower than usual in this hot summer, the shore long and shallow. Keesha was in the deep part, though, and this cat seemed determined to go even deeper.

Keesha imagined how the water must look from the surface— a fog-shrouded expanse, the shore already invisible, the sun barely up and offering only a diffuse glow. All sense of direction would be quickly obliterated for a land animal. The cat seemed to be angling vaguely north, but Keesha suspected he would soon be swimming in circles. *I should stay out of this...*

But when have I ever stayed out of something just because it was none of my business?

Keesha let himself drift higher for a closer look. His eyes widened. *No...*

He made a slow turn around the animal just to be sure. The current he was creating must have been noticeable to the cat, because his swimming became suddenly choppy.

I'd better say hello.

Keesha broke the surface right alongside the swimmer. He was momentarily taken aback by the fact that the cat had some sort of dead animal in his mouth. "Arcove?"

Arcove cut his eyes sideways at Keesha. They were dilated to near-blackness, and Keesha could see the whites. Arcove was trying to pant around the sodden bundle of fur. He sounded like he was choking on it. "What are you doing out here?" asked Keesha. "What is that thing?"

Voices shouted from the shore. More ferryshaft howls. Keesha got a better look at the object Arcove was holding, trailing in the water beside him. "You are carrying a ferryshaft tail... And you are being pursued by a lot of angry ferryshaft. This is interesting. Who did you murder?"

Arcove veered away from him, but Keesha followed easily. "You know you are swimming in circles, right? There are no islands nearby. You are going to drown."

He thought Arcove growled at him, but it might just have been his attempts to breathe.

Keesha sighed. "Give that here, so that you can explain yourself." He tried to catch the end of the tail, and Arcove jerked his head away, turning in a tight circle. Keesha let his long body float up and spiral around them. "Just let go of it for a moment. What is wrong with you? If it sinks, I will bring it back. There is nothing I cannot find in the water. Why are you always so stubborn? Arcove!" Keesha was becoming annoyed. *"Did* you murder someone? Who is this?"

He managed to catch the end of the tail, but Arcove still wouldn't let go. His lips were drawn back, white teeth gleaming. He was snarling and choking. Then, in their struggle, he breathed in water, and went under.

Keesha caught him around the middle and then caught his back feet, too, because he seemed ready to kick. Arcove's front claws sank into his furry coils, and Keesha gritted his teeth. But Arcove wasn't fighting very well. He was struggling to breathe. He was easier to contain than he should have been. He still hadn't let go of the tail.

Keesha's anger evaporated. *You are exhausted and panicking.* He brought his face down in front of Arcove's. Green eyes glared at him over sodden red fur. Keesha forced himself to speak quietly. "Do you remember what you said to me seven years ago? When I fell into the snow bowl in Leeshwood?"

At first, Keesha thought Arcove was too lost inside his own head to even understand words. Then he blinked once. The rhythm of his shallow panting changed.

"You said, 'I am not going to let you die in a snow bowl. Trust me.' Well, *I* am not going to let you die in a lake. Trust me?"

Another blink.

"You have the benefit of doubt from me," continued Keesha patiently. He glanced at the tail. "Whoever that was, they probably deserved it."

To his surprise, Arcove shut his eyes and made a guttural noise that was clearly a sign of distress.

Keesha cocked his head. "Well, you can keep not explaining yourself, and we can float out here all day. Easier, granted, if you take your claws out of me."

The claws vanished at once. Keesha was pleased to see that Arcove was regaining some self-control.

Keesha began humming a song of soothing. He had no idea whether it would work on creasia, but it seemed worth a try. Arcove's chin settled heavily onto his coil. *You are completely worn out, aren't you?*

In moments, he was deadweight. Keesha shifted him around to a more comfortable position. He stared in bafflement at the tail, still clamped in Arcove's jaws. Keesha sighed. He spun in lazy circles, treading water far out in the deep section of the lake. He sang to himself as he watched the sun burn off the mist and wondered what Arcove would say when he woke.

V

Arcove returned to himself as though swimming up from some great depth. For a moment, he thought he was in his den and he would presently go find Roup and hunt, perhaps take a few cubs.

Then he remembered. Charder. The journey to the Ghost Wood. Sedaron. That dead creasia in the grass. Charder's head on his paw… Sadness like physical pain lanced through him. He must have moved or made a noise, because Keesha's face was suddenly right in front of him.

"Arcove?"

Arcove started to say something and realized he was still gripping Charder's tail. Thirst hit him like a hoof blow. His mouth tasted like something dead. Of course it did.

Arcove put a paw over the tail to hold it against Keesha's coil. He let go of it, and immediately began lapping lake water as though he hadn't had a drink in a day. Which he hadn't.

He noted absently that not too much time had passed since he went to sleep. The sun was not even halfway up the sky. He felt sharper, though. In spite of the returning misery of his errand and recent discoveries, he felt like he could think properly again, perhaps even fight properly. *Telshee sleep…*

He finally stopped drinking and looked up. Keesha was watching him with what Arcove thought was probably a worried expression. *I suppose I owe him an explanation.* He cleared his throat. "I promised Charder Ela-ferry that I would take him to the Ghost Wood."

Keesha blinked. He looked at the tail, looked back at Arcove. "Charder is dead?"

"He became sick very suddenly," said Arcove. "He didn't tell anyone until about a month ago."

Keesha was silent a moment. He even stopped humming.

Arcove rested his chin on his paws on top of Keesha's coil. The telshee had generously brought up a coil under his stomach and hindlegs instead of wrapping him up, which made Arcove feel more secure and less trapped. *What am I going to do? They won't let me get near the Ghost Wood.* He'd tried repeatedly over the course of the night, but the ferryshaft had quickly figured out what he wanted.

I said I would never again be outnumbered and surrounded. I made that promise to myself, and I didn't keep it. I'm not making good on any of my promises lately.

Keesha spoke. "You are not sleeping, not drinking. When did you last eat?"

Arcove had not even thought about eating since he went to find Charder. He spoke absently. "I don't remember." He squinted towards the shore. There was a ferryshaft there in the distance, watching. Arcove gritted his teeth. "I was trying to swim to the Ghost Wood when I jumped into the lake. Could you swim me over there? To the area where it touches the water?" It was not Arcove's habit to ask Keesha for favors, but he was beyond caring how he did this, so long as it got done.

Keesha ignored his request. "Do you want to follow Charder into the dark?"

"What? No."

Keesha brought his head down again on a level with Arcove's, his enormous sea monster eyes searching his face. "I am sorry I said that he deserved it."

Arcove looked away. He stared at Charder's tail, dragging in the water, and said, "It is a reasonable assumption that if I am carrying a ferryshaft tail, I have killed that ferryshaft. You could be forgiven for thinking so."

Keesha was no expert at reading emotion in creasia faces, but when it came to tone of voice, he had perfect pitch. "Arcove…"

Far too much pity. Arcove spoke over him. "At any rate, I encountered some old enemies who—"

"I am sorry." Keesha licked the top of his head. This was not actually how telshees offered comfort. It was creasia behavior that Keesha had taken to mimicking. Roup thought it was funny. Arcove found it alarming.

"Ghosts! Please don't do that."

"You sound heartbroken."

"I'm—" Arcove didn't know what he was. He tried to return to the safe haven of a problem that needed solving. "Sedaron has apparently brought ferryshaft from the other side of the Ghost Wood. They've allied with lowland curbs to kill creasia who come here to mourn. They're using the fact that we often come alone, carrying tokens of our dead. We cannot bring ourselves to drop these tokens. It…makes us easy to kill."

A long silence. Keesha was spinning a little faster in the water. He was humming to himself again. The sound had an edge that Arcove thought he recognized. *Have I said the wrong thing?* "Keesha?" Arcove looked up to find his face again. "What are you thinking?"

"I am angry."

"Oh." Arcove found this oddly comforting. "Thank you?"

"This is a vile way to kill an intelligent animal."

Arcove sighed. "I'll do something about it. But right now I *have* to take Charder."

Arcove thought Keesha was going to tell him that Charder's tail was not going anywhere. He would still be dead months or years from now and there was no reason for Arcove to risk another encounter with Sedaron's herd at this moment.

Instead, Keesha said, in a more hesitant voice, "Why do cats do this? Bite off pieces of dead friends and carry them halfway across the island?"

"Yes, I know you think it's violent and primitive," snapped Arcove.

"I am not thinking anything," said Keesha. "I am asking."

Arcove thought for a moment. Keesha already knew what creasia believed about ghosts and the place that ferryshaft called Groth. But Keesha also knew that not all creasia were taken to the Ghost Wood. Cats still believed their ghosts would find a way into that place like water running downhill. The actual journey was important for other reasons.

"The old den mothers tell a story," said Arcove at last. "I don't know whether it's true."

"Tell me?"

"They say that we used to live alone or in pairs and fight each other for territory and mates and food. But when we began to speak, we made friends with each other and we became...attached. This helped us to hunt more efficiently and defend ourselves from other species. But it also made us vulnerable to…grief. Creasia would lose a companion, and they could not convince themselves that their friend was gone. They would keep looking for that cat, month after month, and pine away, and sometimes die. So the den mothers began sending creasia to the Ghost Wood with a token of their dead loved ones. It was a long journey with the scent of death always present. By the time we reached the wood, we were convinced that our friend was truly gone. We were able to stop looking for them around every corner."

Keesha was silent for a long moment. Arcove watched Charder's tail dragging in the water. At last, Keesha said softly, "You creasia seem so simple, but you're not. How can you be so violent and yet love each other so much?"

Arcove didn't have an answer.

"You will feel better if you can take Charder to the Ghost Wood now?"

"Yes."

"Then I will help you, but approach via the lake is not possible. Groth moves quickly by the water. Tendrils wrap and drown animals. Also, the bowls of the plants tip poison into the water along the shore. Not safe for me, not safe for you."

"Oh." Arcove's ears drooped. "You can't go out onto the plain, Keesha. It's too hot and dry. You would weaken quickly. Then they would circle you and kill you just like they are going to do with me."

"I am not letting you out of the water until you come up with a better plan than that," said Keesha mildly.

Arcove thought he should be offended, but he laughed. "You are going to let me do whatever I have to do. I think—"

At that moment, noise and movement erupted near the shore. They were a long way out into the lake, and Arcove's eyes had difficulty with great distances in broad daylight. He craned his head, trying to make sense of the running shapes. "Have the ferryshaft found another mourning creasia to kill?"

Keesha was also blinking and squinting in the bright light. "I do see a creasia," he began. "Maybe two—"

"Arcove!" bellowed a distant voice.

Arcove shot up against Keesha's coil. "Roup?" He was down into the water, nearly forgetting Charder's tail, snatching it at the last moment, swimming as hard as he could.

Keesha hissed behind him. "Do you really think you can outswim me?"

Arcove didn't think anything. He was frantic. Keesha scooped him up, and then there was actual *wind* as Keesha shot across the lake. As they drew closer, the shapes resolved. Roup and Halvery were in the shallows, fighting with at least a dozen ferryshaft. The ferryshaft were having difficulty because Roup and Halvery could protect each other's backs. Critically, they could also use their teeth. Arcove spotted two dead ferryshaft further up the bank beneath the trees, and a wounded animal limping away.

The creasia were injured, too. How badly, Arcove couldn't tell. There was blood in the water. They were being slowly overwhelmed by sheer numbers.

Arcove shook himself free of Keesha and flashed across the last stretch of shallow water. He plowed into the nearest ferryshaft with his claws, catching the animal by surprise and flipping it into the air. Keesha had covered the distance to the shore so rapidly that most of the ferryshaft had not yet seen him. Arcove sent two more reeling by the time the rest realized that a third cat was attacking them.

To their credit, the ferryshaft did not break. Not until Keesha reared out of the lake, opened his great toothy maw and snarled. He made a low, humming note that somehow set every animal's hair on end and seemed to vibrate in the earth beneath their feet. One didn't need to know anything about telshees to recognize this as a threat.

The ferryshaft fled, galloping up the shallow stretch of shore and disappearing into the trees. Halvery caught one thrashing, injured animal in the water and made a swift end of it. Another moved, and he went to take care of that one, too.

Arcove dropped Charder's tail, confident now that Keesha would retrieve it for him. "Roup," he growled as they came nose to nose, "I should box your ears."

"Do it." Roup rubbed his face against Arcove's and then buried his nose against his throat.

Arcove heard himself give a brief, ragged purr, entirely involuntary.

Halvery came splashing back from dispatching the last injured ferryshaft. "When was the last time you boxed his ears?" he asked cheerfully. "Never? That sounds about right."

"I thought they hurt you," whispered Roup, "and then you swam into the lake and drowned."

"I told you to stay in Leeshwood," rumbled Arcove.

"If he's actually in trouble, so am I," said Halvery. "I knew what we were doing."

Arcove sighed. "I have managed to unite my least cooperative officers over concerns for my safety and judgment."

Roup drew back and started washing Arcove's face. Arcove would not normally allow this in front of another officer. Today, he let him. "Were we wrong?" asked Roup.

"I think the answer is self-evident."

Keesha had made a half circle around them and draped Charder's tail over a coil of his body. He raised his head high, watching the shore. "Ferryshaft are coming back."

"Are you two injured?" asked Arcove.

"Bites and bruises," said Halvery, whose left ear was bleeding profusely. "Nothing serious."

Roup looked up at Keesha. "Thank you for not letting him drown."

Keesha shrugged with his coils. "Thank you for helping me out of a snow bowl."

"The only reason you were in that snow bowl is because you were helping us. Again, thank you."

"I am finding creasia more interesting than I expected," said Keesha. "I suppose it is because you only recently began to talk."

Roup rolled his eyes.

"Have the two of you gotten a good look at what Sedaron's herd has been doing?" asked Arcove.

"Killing cats who come to the Ghost Wood," snarled Halvery. "It's contemptible."

"Killing them easily," agreed Arcove, "because they refuse to drop tokens of their dead. The ferryshaft have allied with lowland curbs for this."

"Contemptible," repeated Halvery. "I take it we're going to come back here with all the clutters and have a good old fashioned battle? Perhaps annihilate Sedaron's herd?"

"Maybe." Arcove didn't want to think about that right now. "I have to take Charder to the Ghost Wood. Then I will work on the rest."

He half expected some kind of pushback from Halvery, but he only said, "Sir, that's going to be a challenge."

"I know. You don't have to be involved. This isn't Leeshwood's business. It's mine."

"I know that, sir." He turned to meet Arcove's eyes. "Please believe me when I say that I am honored to be part of your business. Roup trusted me a great deal to bring me along, and I hope he doesn't think he made a mistake."

"I know I didn't," said Roup.

"You almost never do," sighed Arcove. To Halvery, he said, "You're not being a good officer right now. You're being a good friend."

Halvery looked touched. He started to say something, but stopped because a group of ferryshaft had reached the shoreline. There were only three of them this time. One was Sedaron. They stopped at the edge of the trees and waited.

"I believe they want to parley with us," murmured Arcove.

"I doubt they're going to say anything constructive," muttered Roup, "but we might as well hear them."

"They will not come into the water because of me," murmured Keesha. "If you do not venture off the lakebed, I think you are safe."

"So the shoreline is neutral ground," said Arcove. "Very well."

VI

Arcove led the way through the mud and pools until they were within a few paces of Sedaron. The ferryshaft looked hard-eyed and unreadable. His subordinates were a pair of large males who were probably eight or nine years old, born after the rebellion.

Arcove spoke first. "Sedaron Ela-ferry, you are walking very close to total destruction for yourself and your herd. The only way you might avoid catastrophe is by returning to the far side of the Ghost Wood and never showing your face on my side again. Allow me to forget you exist, and I might. Otherwise, you are in for a bloody summer and a bloodier winter. Those are my terms."

Sedaron gave a dry laugh. "Terms," he murmured, "from a trio of cornered cats who can't get out of the water. I spit upon your terms. Here are mine. Give us Charder's tail. He may have been a traitor, but you should not be allowed to desecrate a ferryshaft body no matter who he was. Then I think I will take…a *cull.*" Sedaron's eyes glittered. "One of you will come out and try your luck with us on open ground. We'll have our little fun, and the rest of you can go your way. Pick which friend will die, Arcove. Or come yourself; it doesn't matter to me."

Arcove's eyes narrowed. "How very poetic. Do your followers know that *you* were in favor of the ferryshaft cull? As I recall, you preferred it to any restriction upon your number of mates."

"Do not try to make me the monster," spat Sedaron. "The three of you are still in a supremely precarious position. You should leap at the chance for two to survive."

"You should leap at the chance to avoid my wrath," snapped Arcove, "which is legendary."

Sedaron sniffed. "Do you plan to swim all the way back to Leeshwood? It's a long way, Arcove, and it's daytime. You'll have to stay in deep water to get away from us. Does your telshee ally fancy carrying all three of you?"

"I have carried more," said Keesha cooly. "Do you fancy always looking over your shoulder, Sedaron? I make a very unpleasant enemy."

Sedaron waved his tail. "I remember Kuwee Island, sea snake. You're good at picking the losing side. One would think Arcove, of all animals, would remember that." His eyes shifted back to Arcove. "Know this: even if you somehow survive to return to Leeshwood, your power over my people is ending. News of what you have done to Charder—a ferryshaft who helped you—will run far and wide over the island. Ferryshaft herds will unite and crush you. We are much more numerous now."

Arcove thought that, if he'd been a different kind of person, he would have tried to explain why he was taking Charder's tail to the Ghost Wood. But the idea of sharing his grief and pain with Sedaron was unthinkable. "Ghosts take you," growled Arcove. "It would be kinder than what I'm going to do."

"We will eat your cubs and kill your deer until you starve fighting each other," hissed Sedaron. "We will do to you exactly as you have done to us."

Sedaron continued a litany of threats and grievances, but Arcove was distracted by Roup's tail, which smacked him on the flank so hard that it couldn't possibly be an accident. Arcove glanced at Roup, and Roup's eyes flicked up.

Arcove looked into the tree above Sedaron. It was all he could do to avoid staring and thereby attracting the attention of their enemies.

Storm Ela-ferry was grinning down at them, looking for all the world like a miniature version of Coden. He'd made himself comfortable on a broad limb, but now he got up and looked as though he intended to jump.

"No!" blurted Roup.

Sedaron took this as a horrified response to his threats. "Yes."

Halvery spoke up. "Do you really think you can follow us all the way back to Leeshwood? With only *fifty ferryshaft*?" He glanced up at Storm as he said it.

Sedaron looked a little confused. "I believe that is more than enough to kill you."

Arcove risked another glance at Storm. *There are too many of them; don't join us here.* But Storm didn't look impressed. He jumped.

Sedaron hadn't survived more than fifty years of vicious fighting for nothing. He sensed the movement overhead at the last instant and dodged sideways before Storm's hooves connected with his skull. All three ferryshaft lunged back and Storm landed in the middle, grinning around at them. "Sedaron Ela-ferry... You don't know me, but I feel like I know you."

"I know you well enough," growled Sedaron, clearly shaken, but recovering quickly. One of the other ferryshaft howled, probably to call reinforcements, but the three of them were already calming down. Storm was smaller and apparently alone. "You had your chance to free our kind from creasia influences, Storm Ela-ferry, and you threw it away for the false security of their protection. You sleep in the dens of predators that killed your father and friends. You are a disgrace to your species."

Storm waved his tail. "Spoken like a complete coward. You had, what, twelve years under creasia rule? Twelve years to take action! And all you did was volunteer low-ranking members of the herd for slaughter so that you could keep siring as many foals as you liked. *I* actually challenged Arcove. I actually changed things.

"But I almost wasn't around to do it, Sedaron. I almost died during my first winter, and do you know why? Not cats, no. Ferryshaft. Your foal, specifically. Kelsy and his clique targeted me because I was small and alone and an odd color. They stole my food until I nearly starved. I learned how to be a hunted animal while running from ferryshaft, not creasia. I cut my teeth on your wretched foal. He was a bully, and he learned it from you."

Sedaron made an abrupt lunge at Storm, his teeth snapping, front hooves lashing.

But Storm simply...wasn't there. *He's gotten even faster,* thought Arcove.

Storm was fifteen now, the same age Coden had been on Turis Rock. He was as quick as a summer snake, with an insolent confidence to match.

One of the other young males lunged at him. Storm dodged and then jumped straight into the air as the third attacked. He came down still right beside them, which must have been maddening.

"Kelsy grew up and got better," continued Storm in a voice that was barely winded. "He regretted his behavior. But you're where he learned that behavior, and I don't think you've ever been anything except a scheming bully. You unite your herd with shared hatreds, attack those who haven't provoked you, take food from the weak, and volunteer others for slaughter." Storm's voice dropped to a snarl. "I *loathe* bullies, Sedaron."

"You unnatural, cat-loving abomination," spat Sedaron. "Coden lost a war for the ferryshaft, and you seem bent on losing our dignity!"

"I love quite a few cats," agreed Storm. "I've never cared much about dignity." He whipped in past Sedaron's guard and gave him a slash on the face that bloodied his nose.

All three ferryshaft lunged at Storm, and this time he tore away from them through the trees. Unfortunately, he ran straight into the reinforcements who'd responded to the rally howls. There was a flurry of dust and snarls. For a moment, Arcove thought they'd caught him. Then a pale streak flashed into the sunlight beyond the trees. "Wait for me, creasia!" he shouted over his shoulder. "Just wait!"

Roup laughed.

Halvery shook his ears. "He's going to get himself killed."

"I don't think so," said Roup.

"He's as mad as Coden!"

"He's certainly as fast as Coden," muttered Arcove.

"Storm will be back," said Keesha serenely, "and I think you should do what he says."

"I'm not sure we have much of a choice," said Arcove.

There was a great deal of howling, yipping, and shouting out across the plain. Curbs came trotting along the shoreline twice, glanced at the creasia and telshee, and kept going.

True to his word, Storm came slipping back along his own trail some little while later, walking carefully around the dry leaves. He spoke in a rush, "Arcove, Roup, Halvery, come on. Not you, Keesha; it's too dry."

"Everyone thinks I am very fragile," complained Keesha. "I can leave the water for a little while."

"We'll come back when this is over," said Storm. "Really, it's too dry. Come on, creasia! Let's go for a hunt!"

"You're enjoying this entirely too much," grumbled Halvery. "You can't have led them very far away in that amount of time. They'll see us as soon as we come out of the trees, if not before."

"Of course they will," said Storm. "I only led them around to make them angry."

"Do you have a plan?" asked Arcove. "Because there are a *lot* of them, Storm. Halvery was only guessing at fifty. It might be more. And they have lowland curbs."

"I have a plan," said Storm. "I'd explain, but there's no time. Sedaron's ferryshaft may run across the wrong scent trail at any moment. We need to hurry."

"Halvery is right that they will see us as soon as we leave the trees," said Roup.

"I want them to see us," said Storm. "I want them to chase us. Come on, Arcove! Let's get Charder to the Ghost Wood."

They left the lake at a run. Arcove heard hoofbeats before they even made it through Chelby Wood—shouts and howls, yipping. *I hope you know what you're doing, Storm.*

They emerged from the trees and were immediately cut off by at least a dozen ferryshaft. Storm veered away in the direction of the

Ghost Wood, the three creasia running with him. Arcove realized that he would not be able to match Storm's pace for long. He was a silver ripple through the green grass; he was *flying*.

But the Ghost Wood was so close. Arcove caught sight of the pink, frilly mouths of the ghost plants. He could smell the sweet, strangely beckoning scent. But there were ferryshaft and curbs between them and the wood, and they were already running to intercept Storm and his companions.

Arcove thought about simply hurling Charder's tail into the trees, much as Roup had flung the Shable for Coden. It wasn't the way he'd wanted to do this, but it might be the only way.

Storm jerked left as the ferryshaft closed in. He was running parallel to the Ghost Wood, slowing down. Arcove wondered whether Storm was tired. He didn't look it.

Most of the ferryshaft were behind them at this point, converging. The curbs were further back. Storm slowed a little more.

"Storm?" called Halvery. "They are catching up…"

"Trust me!"

The ferryshaft were right behind them as they topped a little rise and came down the other side of a steep hollow.

There were animals crouching in the hollow. They rose up to meet the unsuspecting pursuers head on. Arcove wasn't surprised to see Sauny and Valla. He wasn't surprised to see Storm's mate, Tollee. But the first animal over the rise wasn't a ferryshaft at all. It was Carmine Ela-creasia, with Teek at his side.

The excited barks and howls behind them turned into yelps and cries of terror. Arcove turned, panting around Charder's tail, to see his cub laying a red path through their pursuers. Storm doubled back and shouted, "Teek, with me!"

They flashed through the chaos of ferryshaft, now in disorderly retreat from Carmine, and made straight for Sedaron at the rear of the group. He saw them coming, turned, and beat an undignified retreat back along the edge of the Ghost Wood. "What's wrong, Sedaron?" bawled Storm, who apparently still had breath for shouting. "The odds are still in your favor! Is three to one not good enough for you?"

Teek chimed in, "I think he only fights cubs and the elderly!"

"That explains it!"

They had nearly caught him when Sedaron veered into the Ghost Wood and vanished. "Ghosts take you," growled Arcove around Charder's tail.

Halvery was fighting with the ferryshaft alongside Carmine. Sauny, Valla, and Tollee were going round and round with six of them in a blur of red and blond tails and flying hooves. Roup had backed up against Arcove.

He felt like he should be helping, but he still couldn't use his teeth, and none of the ferryshaft seemed inclined to come near him now. The curbs were nowhere in sight. Their remaining enemies seemed to lose their nerve all at once. They broke and fled, the creasia and ferryshaft chasing after them, killing stragglers, until the group vanished among the ghost plants.

"They've got a trail," panted Storm, who finally seemed winded. "I've never...never seen that before."

He was right. There was a narrow, but clear path winding away among the ghost plants. Their upper bowls and tendrils overshadowed it so that the trail seemed more like a tunnel than a path. Storm stuck his head inside, sniffing. Tollee said, in a warning voice, "Storm..."

"I'm not going to follow them. I just..."

"Storm!"

"Alright, alright. Curbs have come this way, along with the ferryshaft. I can smell them. They must have some technique for keeping it clear. That must be how they came through from the other side."

"How does it not close?" wondered Teek.

"I'm going in," said Sauny.

"No," said Valla flatly, "you are not."

The group continued to argue and speculate.

Arcove turned away. He would worry about Sedaron's herd and trails through the Ghost Wood later. Right now, he needed to fulfill his purpose in coming here before anything else went wrong. He turned west to choose a spot at some distance from Sedaron's tunnel.

Roup followed him, but the rest did not notice their departure for a moment.

"Wait!"

Arcove turned to see them all hurrying to catch up. "We came to help you," said Storm. "Wait for us."

Arcove had not expected to have an audience. He hadn't wanted one. Feeling a little uncertain, he stopped beside a glossy bowl with bright pink frills around its edges. The water inside gave off a heady perfume.

Arcove slid Charder's tail into the bowl. He stared into the sticky water for a long moment, feeling both a sense of relief and a sense of lost purpose. The only tradition here was to say the animal's name. Beyond that, cats did whatever felt right to them.

Arcove spoke slowly, "Charder Ela-ferry...you became one of my officers so slowly that neither of us knew when it happened. You stood with me on Kuwee Island when all hope was lost. You taught me to read. You forgave a great deal. You were a good councilor and a good friend. I will miss you more than I think you would believe."

Arcove kept his eyes on the ghost plant as he spoke. He almost forgot his audience, but as he finished, he became conscious of their absolute silence and stillness. He wondered whether they were embarrassed to be here, whether they thought he was making a fool of himself. *Well, you all invited yourselves along on something that was none of your business.*

"He was my herd leader," said Storm suddenly. "He saved my mother and my grandmother, so that I could exist. He asked Pathar to train me when nobody in the herd wanted anything to do with me. And he made my mother very happy for the last nine years. Goodbye, Charder. You forgave a great deal, and so you are also forgiven. Be at peace, old friend."

"Goodbye, Charder," murmured Teek, and the words ran round the group.

"Goodbye, Charder. Goodbye, Goodbye."

"Tell Pathar I miss him," said Storm.

A smile crept into Roup's voice as he whispered, "Tell Coden we said hello."

Arcove settled back on his haunches, a sense of emptiness replacing the cold rock in his stomach. He realized that he was lightheaded with hunger.

Storm spoke beside him. "Arcove, why did you leave like that? We would have all come with you. My mother wanted to talk to you. She wanted to thank you."

"For what?" muttered Arcove. "Tormenting him for sixteen years?"

"Arcove!"

He turned to look at Storm. His gray eyes were *so* like Coden's.

"You purred him to sleep."

Arcove swallowed.

"He was so happy you came." Storm's eyes searched his face. "He died with his head on your paw."

And there was the pain again. Sharp, intolerable. Arcove turned away. But Sauny had come up on the other side of him. Ferryshaft were all around him. "We would have all come with you to the Ghost Wood, Arcove. Mother wanted to talk to you a little more. It seemed like you had a hard time carrying on conversations while you were purring. And you never stopped. Not from the time he asked until he died. We all knew when he was gone because you went quiet. And it was the middle of the night, so we all went to sleep. When we woke up in the morning, you'd taken his tail and left. I wish you had waited for us."

Arcove licked his lips. "I thought you might...change your minds. You might find this practice...disturbing, and I promised him—"

Sauny leaned against his shoulder. "Yes, yes, you always keep your promises. But you know he asked you to do this *for you,* right? He asked because he knew this journey would mean something to *you.* But you already did the thing that mattered to Charder, Arcove."

"And it was the kindest thing I have ever seen in my life," added Storm.

Arcove could not meet their eyes, but the sharpness in his chest had eased a little. "I will go back and speak with So-fet," he said quietly. "Or she can come visit my den. I'll make sure no one bothers her."

"I'm sure she'll come when she can," said Storm, "although she's currently watching Tollee's and my spring foal, Valla's two-year-old, and Wisteria's cubs."

Arcove chuffed. His voice became serious again as he said, "I'm afraid the version of this story that is going to spread from Sedaron's herd will do damage to ferryshaft/creasia relations. It is unfortunate that he knew Charder well enough to identify his tail. He'll soon have half the island thinking I killed him."

Tollee gave a mocking laugh from the other side of Storm. "Oh, that'll be pretty difficult."

Arcove glanced at her. "You don't think anyone will believe that I killed a well-loved ferryshaft and carried his tail across the island as a trophy? I know you are currently treating me like a dear, senile uncle, but you do remember who I actually am, don't you?"

Sauny shook with laughter. She had the temerity to lean up and lick his muzzle. Arcove tried to growl, but he just didn't have it in him at the moment. Instead, he said, "Grief is a temporary state; I will recover."

"I hope so," said Sauny. "It's hard to watch you suffer."

"I find that difficult to believe."

"Believe it."

"Ever since the rebellion," said Storm, "ferryshaft have whispered that you only stopped killing us because Keesha forced you to. They say that you are not in a position to attack us again, and that is the only reason you are not still killing ferryshaft. Arcove, I don't know whether you realize how many friends Charder had or how many animals were drifting in and out of his cave two nights ago, but there were quite a few. They came from herds all over the island, and what they saw...well, they'll never say those things about you again."

Arcove fidgeted. "I did not do what I did for a spectacle..."

"That was extremely obvious," said Storm.

"The upshot," said Valla, "is that Sedaron's story is going to run straight into the truth, spreading in the opposite direction. He will unintentionally corroborate what happened by confirming that you actually did take Charder to the Ghost Wood, not to desecrate his body, but to honor him. There will be no damage to ferryshaft/creasia relations and no support at all for some kind of organized attack on Leeshwood. You'll have plenty of assistance from the herds in eliminating these attacks around the Ghost Wood."

Arcove perked up a little.

Sauny grinned at him. "That's the good news. The bad news is that you may have permanently damaged your reputation as a remorseless predator."

"Obliterated," said Storm. "I think he's obliterated it."

Arcove grumbled under his breath. He wondered what on earth Carmine and Teek must think of this conversation. To say nothing of Halvery. Roup was probably laughing.

Arcove got up and shook himself. He turned and started for the lake. "You'll find I'm thoroughly capable of restoring my reputation as a remorseless predator."

"Yes, but why?" asked Sauny, trotting beside him. "Would it be so awful if they honored your wishes because they love you and not because they fear you?"

Arcove lashed his tail. "Fear is reliable. When animals fear you, they do what you say. When they love you, they do things like follow you halfway across the island, even when you told them not to." He shot a glare at Roup.

"They do things like travel all day and half the night to make sure you're safe," agreed Storm.

Arcove sighed. "Thank you. You must have come as soon as you woke up."

"We did. We were able to find Teek and Wisteria and Carmine because they were visiting the Ferryshaft Cave of Histories."

"Where *is* Wisteria?" asked Roup suddenly. "She's as good in a fight as Carmine."

"She is not!" objected Carmine from farther back. "I pin her every time!"

"Only because she lets you!" returned Roup sweetly.

Teek trotted up beside Roup. "We had some trouble on the way. We stayed on the common trail through Leeshwood, but it was muddled in one place, and some dens seemed to be fighting over it."

"They were what!?" exploded Halvery.

"Yes, it was in your territory—"

"I told them…!" Halvery fumed. "Oh, there is going to be blood when I get back."

"I don't think that'll be necessary," said Teek. "Lyndi was sorting it out and Wisteria stayed to help her."

Halvery looked further dismayed. "Lyndi was in my territory… sorting out my dens' issues?"

"Well, yes, she is the highest ranking officer in Leeshwood right now. She's effectively king."

Halvery sputtered.

"Anyway," continued Teek, "Wist is good at this sort of thing. She just talks at cats for a while, and they sort of give up. It's what she does every time some male wants to fight us for her. She takes him aside and talks to him for a long time, and eventually he leaves shaking his head. Anyway, she was helping Lyndi, and they both seemed to think it was important to get the path straightened out, so we left them to it."

Halvery looked like he had swallowed something unpleasant. Roup was smiling.

Arcove yawned. He definitely felt lighter. *But I don't know about this 'loved' thing.* Aloud, he said, "I am so hungry that I am sorely tempted to eat one of these ferryshaft you've killed, but I will restrain myself out of respect for present company."

"There's easy fishing in the lake," said Sauny. "Stranded fish all along the shore."

"And we need to tell Keesha what happened," said Storm. "He was frustrated to be left out."

"Keesha is in the lake?" asked Valla in delight.

"Yes, he kept Arcove from drowning."

"There's another animal who loves you," said Sauny with a smirk.

Arcove chuffed. "He loves me the way a cub loves his favorite chew toy."

"A little like that, yes."

"We have to tell him that Charder said you sing like a telshee," said Valla.

"Please don't."

"He'll want you to do it again."

"The answer is no."

160

Arcove glanced over his shoulder. Roup was walking just behind him, talking to Halvery. Carmine and Teek were a little further back, chatting away. None of them were staring at him. No one seemed shocked that he was padding along surrounded by chattering ferryshaft, two of them Coden's foals.

Arcove thought, *If Charder's ghost is watching, he's smiling.* And that made Arcove smile, too.

VII

Roup lay stretched in the shade, his mind at peace and his stomach full of fish. He was trying not to laugh as he listened to Keesha's attempts to get Arcove to talk about purring. "You sang someone to sleep? You did this?"

"For the last time, I did not sing. Creasia do not sing."

"The ferryshaft say that it sounds like singing. A lullaby, a song for sleep. I would call that singing. I did not know that creasia could do this. How did I not know?"

"Probably because no cat has ever been inspired to purr in your presence."

"Storm says you can talk and also sing at the same time."

"Poorly, but, yes."

"Do it?" Keesha sounded like a cub, begging for a mouse hunt. "I must hear it. Please?"

Arcove was becoming flustered. "I can't...do it on command!"

"Why not?"

"Because...I have to be...actually feeling things; Keesha, can you stop talking about this?"

"I will come by your den. Can you do it there?"

"I don't know. Maybe." Arcove came over and lay down beside Roup. Keesha had the good sense not to follow him. The ferryshaft were chasing each other in the shallow water, catching fish and laughing. It was their time to be awake, and the day was pristine.

Arcove tucked his head against Roup's shoulder and muttered, "Why did they tell him about the purring?"

"Because they love you."

"I think I prefer fear."

"No, you don't."

Halvery was still catching fish with Teek and Carmine. Roup suspected that he was trying to tactfully extract information about how much meddling Lyndi and Wisteria had done in his territory. *Let it go, Halvery.*

Arcove was relaxed and warm against his side. The sunlight through the dappled leaves was pleasant. Roup felt almost safe enough to flop over onto his back. He was dozing when someone said, "Sir?"

Roup opened his eyes.

Carmine was crouching in front of Arcove. "Carmine."

"Sir, I wanted to talk to you about something." He sounded serious and a little nervous.

Arcove sat up.

"I know there's a rumor going around that I intend to challenge you."

Arcove went still.

Roup watched them. Arcove and Carmine were nearly the same size and could have been mistaken for each other at a distance. Teek was standing a little way back, watching the exchange just as closely as Roup.

"I wanted you to know," continued Carmine, "that I won't. That I wouldn't...hurt you, sir."

Arcove stared at him for a long beat. "I see."

"I don't know who will rule Leeshwood after you're gone, but I hope that doesn't happen for a long time. Please don't...think that I'm waiting to pounce on you."

Arcove gave Carmine another long look. "You don't want to hurt me," he repeated. "Right..." Arcove stood up. "Come on, Carmine."

Carmine took a step back, looking confused.

Arcove gave him a too-bright smile. "You and me. Let's go."

"I didn't..."

"You didn't challenge me, no. This is just sparring. Come on."

Arcove started towards a clear spot among the trees. Carmine's tail was twitching. He glanced over at Teek, and now Roup could see his excitement. He whispered, "Really?!"

Teek looked like he was holding in a laugh. "Well, don't keep him waiting."

Carmine went bounding after Arcove and then forced himself to slow to a more dignified walk. Halvery came trotting over from the lakebed, looking interested. The ferryshaft saw that something was happening and came to watch as well.

Roup got up and joined Teek on the edge of the circle. "What do you think will happen?" he whispered.

Teek gave him an assessing look and then the hint of a smile. "I think my dear friend is about to learn humility."

Carmine certainly started off with a great deal of confidence. The two cats circled each other a few times, taking each other's measure. Then they closed like lightning and went over in a blur of flying tails and tufts of black fur.

Arcove came up on top, but this was clearly Carmine's intent. He lashed out with his back claws to deliver a devastating kick to Arcove's stomach.

Arcove flipped him again. This time, he pinned Carmine cross-wise, so that his back legs kicked harmlessly. Arcove held his throat until he stopped struggling.

Halvery gave an appreciative rumble. "And *that* is how it's done."

Carmine got to his feet, looking dazed. "How did you do that?"

"Again?" asked Arcove cheerfully.

"Yes!"

They went again. This time, the fight lasted a little longer and Carmine almost pinned Arcove behind his head, but Arcove flipped him over his shoulders and pinned him cross-wise once more.

The third time, Roup could tell Arcove was winded. When he finally forced Carmine's head to the ground, he stepped away and said, between pants, "Now I'm tired and you're not. Now you could probably kill me. Except, if we were really fighting, I would have already killed you three times over."

Carmine stared up at him with a mixture of injured pride and naked wonder. "How did you do that cross-pin?" he demanded.

Arcove just smiled at him.

Carmine turned to Teek, who flicked his tail. "I was watching, my friend, and I can't tell you how he did it."

"Roup?" demanded Carmine. Roup was his immediate superior, and they were on more personal terms than he and Arcove.

"If you think I discuss my king's fighting techniques with others, you have mistaken me," said Roup coolly.

"Oh, come on!"

Carmine turned back to Arcove. He sagged a little. Roup could see him swallowing his bruised dignity and putting those feelings away. *Good cub.*

"I'm sorry that I couldn't beat you, sir," said Carmine. "I wanted to beat you, because...I wanted you to know that it's safe to get old."

Arcove blinked. He started to say something, stopped. He looked like he might say something serious, but then settled on humor. "Well, you will just have to save that condescension for another time."

Carmine looked a little anxious.

Arcove leaned forward and licked the top of his head. Almost too quietly to hear, he said, "You are such a good cub, Carmine. You'll manage that cross-pin eventually."

Carmine brightened at once. "How did you do it?" He fairly vibrated.

Arcove turned away. "Maybe you'll figure it out next time we spar."

"Arcove!"

Arcove gave a flick of his tail. "Come talk to me about your den. I have some questions about how Wisteria is handling these older challengers of yours. You, too, Teek." They both got up and scampered after him.

The ferryshaft were whispering among themselves. "He's faster than Storm when he wants to be."

"No, he isn't."

"Yes, he is, but he can't keep it up. That's just cats. They sprint."

"Sauny, how *did* you survive running into him when you were only a yearling?"

Sauny, sounding like Coden at his cheekiest: "Immense skill."

Valla's laughter. "Immense luck!"

A snort from Sauny. "Not even that, actually. Just telshees."

Halvery came over and stretched out beside Roup. "Well, I suppose this business with the common way trail will be sorted by the time I get home. I don't know what to think of it."

"You should think of it as a solution to your other problem," said Roup. "If females can rule Leeshwood and handle squabbles outside their territory, no one will fault you for letting your mates sort out a minor question about a challenger for Ilsa."

Halvery cocked his head. "How's that?"

Roup spoke patiently. "If Lyndi can do Arcove's business for a couple of days, Velta can do yours. No shame."

"Oh…" Halvery thought for a moment. "I suppose that's… Roup, you're so good at this. I know where Wisteria gets it. Maybe she's the next king and not Carmine."

Roup smiled and rested his head on his paws.

"But what will be left for us if females are ruling Leeshwood and settling den disputes?"

Roup yawned and stretched. "I suppose you'll have nothing to do except sire hundreds of cubs and take them fishing."

Halvery chuffed. "I suppose *you'll* have nothing to do but look pretty and spar with Arcove."

Roup grinned at him.

Halvery grinned back.

"I can think of worse ways to spend the next twenty years," said Roup.

"So can I."

Made in the USA
Las Vegas, NV
07 February 2022

43282820R00111